Creation Myths and Tales of Origin

Michelle McLaughlin

Copyright © 2013 Michelle McLaughlin

All rights reserved.

ISBN: 1492937029
ISBN-13: 978-1492937029

CONTENTS

1	Blackfoot Creation and Origin Myths	Pg 1
2	Paiute Creation and Origin Legends	Pg 7
3	A Chinese Creation and Flood Myth	Pg 9
4	Creation Myths from the Philippines	Pg 12
5	The Creation of the Earth and the Great Flood	Pg 24
6	Kabyl Creation and Origin Myths	Pg 29
7	The Creation of Life on Earth: A Modern Day Creation Story	Pg 38
8	How the World Began	Pg 41
9	The Creation of Heaven and Earth	Pg 51
10	Legendary Origins	Pg 58
11	The Origin of Underground People: Legends About Elves and Other Hidden Creatures	Pg 67
12	Eve's Unequal Children	Pg 72
13	The Norse Creation Myth	Pg 75

1 BLACKFOOT CREATION AND ORIGIN MYTHS

THE MAKING OF THE EARTH

During the flood, Old Man was sitting on the highest mountain with all the beasts. The flood was caused by the above people, because the baby (a fungus) of the woman who married a star was heedlessly torn in pieces by an Indian child.

Old Man sent the Otter down to get some earth. For a long time he waited, then the Otter came up dead. Old Man examined its feet, but found nothing on them. Next he sent Beaver down, but after a long time he also came up drowned. Again nothing was found on his feet. He sent Muskrat to dive next. Muskrat also was drowned.

At length he sent the Duck. It was drowned, but in its paw held some earth. Old Man saw it, put it in his hand, feigned putting it on the water three times, and at last dropped it. Then the above-people sent rain, and everything grew on the earth.

LANGUAGES CONFUSED ON A MOUNTAIN

After the flood, Old Man mixed water with different colors. He whistled, and all the people came together.

He gave one man a cup of one kind of water, saying, "You will be chief of these people here."

To another man he gave differently colored water, and so on. The Blackfoot, Piegan, and Blood all received black water.

Then he said to the people, "Talk," and they all talked differently; but those who drank black water spoke the same.

This happened on the highest mountain in the Montana Reservation.

ORDER OF LIFE AND DEATH

There was once a time when there were but two persons in the world, Old Man and Old Woman. One time, when they were traveling about, Old Man met Old Woman, who said, "Now, let us come to an agreement of some kind; let us decide how the people shall live."

"Well," said Old Man, "I am to have the first say in everything."

To this Old Woman agreed, provided she had the second say.

Then Old Man began, "The women are to tan the hides. When they do this, they are to rub brains on them to make them soft; they are to scrape them well with scraping tools, etc. But all this they are to do very quickly, for it will not be very hard work."

"No, I will not agree to this," said Old Woman. "They must tan the hide in the way you say; but it must be made very hard work, and take a long time, so that the good workers may be found out."

"Well", said Old Man, "let the people have eyes and mouths in their faces; but they shall be straight up and down."

"No," said Old Woman, "we will not have them that way. We will have the eyes and mouth in the faces, as you say; but they shall all be set crosswise."

"Well," said Old Man, "the people shall have ten fingers on each hand."

"Oh, no!" said Old Woman. "That will be too many. They will be in the way. There shall be four fingers and one thumb on each hand."

"Well," said Old Man, "we shall beget children. The genitals shall be at our navels."

"No," said Old Woman, "that will make childbearing too easy; the people will not care for their children. The genitals shall be at the pubes."

So they went on until they had provided for everything in the lives of the people that were to be. Then Old Woman asked what they should do about life and death.

Should the people always live, or should they die? They had some difficulty in agreeing on this; but finally Old Man said, "I will tell you what I will do. I will throw a buffalo chip into the water, and, if it floats, the people die for four days and live again. But, if it sinks, they will die forever."

So he threw it in, and it floated.

"No," said Old Woman, "we will not decide in that way. I will throw in this rock. If it floats, the people will die for four days. If it sinks, the people will die forever."

Then Old Woman threw the rock out into the water, and it sank to the bottom.

"There," said she, "it is better for the people to die forever; for, if they did not die forever, they would never feel sorry for each other, and there would be no sympathy in the world."

"Well," said Old Man, let it be that way."

After a time Old Woman had a daughter, who died. She was very sorry now that it had been fixed so that people died forever. So she said to Old Man, "Let us have our say over again."

"No," said he, "we fixed it once."

WHY PEOPLE DIE FOREVER

One time Old Man said to Old Woman, "People will never die."

Oh!" said Old Woman, "that will never do; because, if people live always, there will be too many people in the world."

"Well," said, Old Man, "we do not want to die forever. We shall die for four days and then come to life again."

"Oh, no!" said Old Woman, "it will be better to die forever, so that we shall be sorry for each other."

"Well," said Old Man, "we will decide this way. We will throw a buffalo chip into the water. If it sinks, we will die forever; if it floats, we shall live again."

"Well," said Old Woman, "throw it in."

Now, Old Woman had great power, and she caused the chip to turn into a stone, so it sank. So when we die, we die forever.

THE FIRST MARRIAGE

Now in those days, the men and the women did not live together. The men lived in one camp and the women in the other. The men lived in lodges made of skin with the hair on; the women, in good lodges. [The idea is that the women dress the skins, hence the men could not live in dressedskin lodges.] One day Old Man came to the camp of the men, and, when he was there, a woman came over from the camp of the women. She said she had been sent by the chief of the women to invite all the men, because the women were going to pick out husbands.

Now the men began to get ready, and Old Man dressed himself up in his finest clothes. He was always fine looking. Then they started out, and when they came to the women's camp they all stood up in a row.

Now the chief of the women came out to make the first choice. She had on very dirty clothes, and none of the men knew who she was. She went along the line, looked them over, and finally picked out Old Man because of his fine appearance.

Now Old Man saw many nicely dressed women waiting their turn, and when the chief of the women took him by the hand he pulled back and broke away. He did this because he thought her a very common woman. When he pulled away, the chief of the women went back to her lodge and instructed the other women not to choose Old Man.

While the other women were picking out their husbands, the chief of the women put on her best costume. When she came out, she looked very fine, and as soon as Old Man saw her, he thought, "Oh! There is the chief of the women. I wish to be her husband." He did not know that it was the same woman.

Now the chief of the women came down once more to pick out a husband, and as she went around, Old Man kept stepping in front of her, so that she might see him. But she paid no attention to him, finally picking out another for her husband.

After a while all the men had been picked out except Old Man. Now he was very angry; but the chief of the women said to him, "After this you are to be a tree, and stand just where you are now."

Then he became a tree, and he is mad yet, because he is always caving down the bank.

OLD MAN LEADS A MIGRATION

The first Indians were on the other side of the ocean, and Old Man decided to lead them to a better place. So he brought them over the ice to the far north. When they were crossing the ice, the Sarcee were in the middle and there was a boy riding on a dog travois. As they were going along, this boy saw a horn of some animal sticking up through the ice. Now the boy wanted this horn, and began to cry. So his mother took an ax and cut it off. As she did so, the ice gave way, and only those on this side of the place where the horn was will ever get here.

Now Old Man led these people down to where the Blood Reserve now is, and told them that this would be a fine country for them, and that they would be very rich.

He said, "I will get all the people here."

All the people living there ate and lived like wild animals; but Old Man went among them and taught them all the arts of civilization. (When crossing the ice, only about thirty lodges succeeded in getting across, and among these were the representatives of all the tribes now in this country. At that time the Blackfoot were just one tribe.)

When he was through teaching them, he did not die, but went among the Sioux, where he remained for a time, but finally disappeared . He took his wife with him. He had no children.

OLD MAN AND THE GREAT SPIRIT

There was once a Great Spirit who was good. He made a man and a woman. Then Old Man came along. No one made Old Man. He always existed.

The Great Spirit said to him, "Old Man, have you any power?"

"Yes," said Old Man, "I am very strong."

"Well," said the Great Spirit, "suppose you make some mountains."

So Old Man set to work and made the Sweet-Grass Hills. To do this he took a piece of Chief Mountain. He brought Chief Mountain up to its present location, shaped it up, and named it. The other mountains were called blood colts.

"Well," said the Great Spirit, "you are strong."

"Now," said Old Man, "there are four of us: the man and woman, you and I."

The Great Spirit said, "All right."

The Great Spirit said, "I will make a big cross for you to carry."

Old Man said "No, you make another man so that he can carry it."

The Great Spirit made another man. Old Man carried the cross a while, but soon got tired and wanted to go. The Great Spirit told him that he could go, but he should go out among the people and the animals, and teach them how to live, etc.

Now the other man got tired of carrying, the cross. He was a white man. The Great Spirit sent him off as a traveler. So he wandered on alone.

The man and woman who had been created wandered off down towards Mexico, where they tried to build a mountain in order to get to the sky to be with their children. But the people got mixed up until they came to have many different languages.

2 PAIUTE CREATION AND ORIGIN LEGENDS

SOUTHERN PAIUTE LEGEND

Si-chom-pa Ka-gon (Old Woman of the Sea) came out of the sea with a sack filled with something, and securely tied. Then she went back to the home of the Shin-au-av brothers. She delivered to them the sack and told them to carry it to the middle of the world and open it. There they would meet Tov-wots, who would tell them what to do with it. Shin-au-av-pa-vits (the elder) gave the sack to Shin-au-av-skaits (the younger) and told him to do as Si-chom-pa Ka-gon had directed, and especially enjoined upon him that he must not open the sack lest some calamity should befall him.

As he proceeded, his curiosity overcame him, and he untied the sack, when out sprang hosts of people who passed out on the plain, shouting and running toward the mountain.

Then Tov-wots suddenly appeared, being very angry. "Why have you done this? I wanted these people to live in that good land to the east, and here, foolish boy, you have let them out in a desert."

PAIUTE LEGEND OF BRYCE CANYON

Before there were any Indians the Legend People, To-when-an-ung-wa, lived in that place. Because they were bad, Coyote turned them all into rocks. You can see them in that place now -- some standing in rows, some sitting down, some holding onto others. You can see their faces with paint on, just as they were before they became rocks.

    The name of that place is Agka-ku-wass-a-wits (red painted faces).

3 A CHINESE CREATION AND FLOOD MYTH (FROM THE MIAO PEOPLE)

The Miao have no written records, but they have many legends in verse, which they learn to repeat and sing. The Hei Miao (or Black Miao, so called from their dark chocolate-colored clothes) treasure poetical legends of the creation and of a deluge. These are composed in lines of five syllables, in stanzas of unequal length, one interrogative and one responsive. They are sung or recited by two persons or two groups at feasts and festivals, often by a group of youths and a group of maidens. The legend of the creation commences:

> Who made heaven and earth?
> Who made insects?
> Who made men?
> Made male and made female?
> I who speak don't know.

> Heavenly King made heaven and earth,
> Ziene made insects,
> Ziene made men and demons,
> Made male and made female.
> How is it you don't know?

> How made heaven and earth?
> How made insects?

> How made men and demons?
> Made male and made female?
> I who speak don't know.
>
> Heavenly King was intelligent,
> Spat a lot of spittle into his hand,
> Clapped his hands with a noise,
> Produced heaven and earth,
> Tall grass made insects,
> Stories made men and demons,
> Made men and demons,
> Made male and made female.
> How is it you don't know?

The legend proceeds to state how and by whom the heavens were propped up and how the sun was made and fixed in its place.

The legend of the flood tells of a great deluge. It commences:

> Who came to the bad disposition,
> To send fire and burn the hill?
> Who came to the bad disposition,
> To send water and destroy the earth?
> I who sing don't know.
>
> Zie did. Zie was of bad disposition,
> Zie sent fire and burned the hill;
> Thunder did. Thunder was of bad disposition,
> Thunder sent water and destroyed the earth.
> Why don't you know?

In this story of the flood only two persons were saved in a large bottle gourd used as a boat, and these were A-Zie and his sister. After the flood the brother wished his sister to become his wife, but she objected to this as not being proper. At length she proposed that one should take the upper and one the lower millstone, and going to opposite hills should set the stones rolling to the valley between. If these should be found in the valley properly adjusted on above the other, she would be his wife, but not if they came to rest apart.

The young man, considering it unlikely that two stones thus rolled down from opposite hills would be found in the valley, one upon another, while pretending to accept the test suggested, secretly placed two other stones in the valley, one upon the other. The stones rolled from the hills were lost in the tall wild grass, and on descending into the valley, A-Zie called his sister to come and see the stones he had placed.

She, however, was not satisfied, and suggested as another test that each should take a knife from a double sheath and, going again to the opposite hilltops, hurl them into the valley below. If both these knives were found in the sheath in the valley, she would marry him, but if the knives were found apart, they would live apart.

Again the brother surreptitiously placed two knives in the sheath, and, the experiment ending as A-Zie wished, his sister became his wife. They had one child, a misshapen thing without arms or legs, which A-Zie in great anger killed and cut to pieces. He threw the pieces all over the hill, and next morning, on awakening, he found these pieces transformed into men and women. Thus the earth was re-peopled.

4 CREATION MYTHS FROM THE PHILIPPINES

HOW THE WORLD WAS MADE

This is the ancient Filipino account of the creation.

Thousands of years ago there was no land nor sun nor moon nor stars, and the world was only a great sea of water, above which stretched the sky. The water was the kingdom of the god Maguayan, and the sky was ruled by the great god Captan.

Maguayan had a daughter called Lidagat, the sea, and Captan had a son known as Lihangin, the wind. The gods agreed to the marriage of their children, so the sea became the bride of the wind.

Three sons and a daughter were born to them. The sons were called Licalibutan, Liadlao, and Libulan; and the daughter received the name of Lisuga.

Licalibutan had a body of rock and was strong and brave; Liadlao was formed of gold and was always happy; Libulan was made of copper and was weak and timid; and the beautiful Lisuga had a body of pure silver and was sweet and gentle. Their parents were very fond of them, and nothing was wanting to make them happy.

After a time Lihangin died and left the control of the winds to his eldest son Licalibutan. The faithful wife Lidagat soon followed her husband, and the children, now grown up, were left without father or mother. However, their grandfathers, Captan and Maguayan, took care of them and guarded them from all evil.

After a time, Licalibutan, proud of his power over the winds, resolved to gain more power, and asked his brothers to join him in an attack on Captan in the sky above. At first they refused; but when Licalibutan became angry with them, the amiable Liadlao, not wishing to offend his brother, agreed to help. Then together they induced the timid Libulan to join in the plan.

When all was ready the three brothers rushed at the sky, but they could not beat down the gates of steel that guarded the entrance. Then Licalibutan let loose the strongest winds and blew the bars in every direction. The brothers rushed into the opening, but were met by the angry god Captan. So terrible did he look that they turned and ran in terror; but Captan, furious at the destruction of his gates, sent three bolts of lightning after them.

The first struck the copper Libulan and melted him into a ball. The second struck the golden Liadlao, and he too was melted. The third bolt struck Licalibutan, and his rocky body broke into many pieces and fell into the sea. So huge was he that parts of his body stuck out above the water and became what is known as land.

In the meantime the gentle Lisuga had missed her brothers and started to look for them. She went toward the sky, but as she approached the broken gates, Captan, blind with anger, struck her too with lightning, and her silver body broke into thousands of pieces.

Captan then came down from the sky and tore the sea apart, calling on Maguayan to come to him and accusing him of ordering the attack on the sky. Soon Maguayan appeared and answered that he knew nothing of the plot as he had been asleep far down in the sea.

After a time he succeeded in calming the angry Captan. Together they wept at the loss of their grandchildren, especially the gentle and beautiful Lisuga; but with all their power they could not restore the dead to life. However, they gave to each body a beautiful light that will shine forever.

And so it was that golden Liadlao became the sun, and copper Libulan the moon, while the thousands of pieces of silver Lisuga shine as the stars of heaven. To wicked Licalibutan the gods gave no light, but resolved to make his body support a new race of people. So Captan gave Maguayan a seed, and he planted it on the land, which, as you will remember, was part of Licalibutan's huge body.

Soon a bamboo tree grew up, and from the hollow of one of its branches a man and a woman came out. The man's name was Sicalac, and the woman was called Sicabay. They were the parents of the human race. Their first child was a son whom they called Libo; afterwards they had a daughter who was known as Saman. Pandaguan was a younger son and he had a son called Arion.

Pandaguan was very clever and invented a trap to catch fish. The very first thing he caught was a huge shark. When he brought it to land, it looked so great and fierce that he thought it was surely a god, and he at once ordered his people to worship it. Soon all gathered around and began to sing and pray to the shark. Suddenly the sky and sea opened, and the gods came out and ordered Pandaguan to throw the shark back into the sea and to worship none but them.

All were afraid except Pandaguan. He grew very bold and answered that the shark was as big as the gods, and that since he had been able to overpower it he would also be able to conquer the gods. Then Captan, hearing this, struck Pandaguan with a small thunderbolt, for he did not wish to kill him but merely to teach him a lesson. Then he and Maguayan decided to punish these people by scattering them over the earth, so they carried some to one land and some to another. Many children were afterwards born, and thus the earth became inhabited in all parts.

Pandaguan did not die. After lying on the ground for thirty days he regained his strength, but his body was blackened from the lightning, and all his descendants ever since that day have been black.

His first son, Arion, was taken north, but as he had been born before his father's punishment he did not lose his color, and all his people therefore are white.

Libo and Saman were carried south, where the hot sun scorched their bodies and caused all their descendants to be of a brown color.

A son of Saman and a daughter of Sicalac were carried east, where the land at first was so lacking in food that they were compelled to eat clay. On this account their children and their children's children have always been yellow in color.

And so the world came to be made and peopled. The sun and moon shine in the sky, and the beautiful stars light up the night. All over the land, on the body of the envious Licalibutan, the children of Sicalac and Sicabay have grown great in numbers. May they live forever in peace and brotherly love!

THE CREATION (IGOROT)

In the beginning there were no people on the earth.

Lumawig, the Great Spirit, came down from the sky and cut many reeds. He divided these into pairs which he placed in different parts of the world, and then he said to them, "You must speak."

Immediately the reeds became people, and in each place was a man and a woman who could talk, but the language of each couple differed from that of the others.

Then Lumawig commanded each man and woman to marry, which they did. By and by there were many children, all speaking the same language as their parents. These, in turn, married and had many children. In this way there came to be many people on the earth.

Now Lumawig saw that there were several things which the people on the earth needed to use, so he set to work to supply them. He created salt, and told the inhabitants of one place to boil it down and sell it to their neighbors. But these people could not understand the directions of the Great Spirit, and the next time he visited them, they had not touched the salt.

Then he took it away from them and gave it to the people of a place called Mayinit. These did as he directed, and because of this he told them that they should always be owners of the salt, and that the other peoples must buy of them.

Then Lumawig went to the people of Bontoc and told them to get clay and make pots. They got the clay, but they did not understand the molding, and the jars were not well shaped. Because of their failure, Lumawig told them that they would always have to buy their jars, and he removed the pottery to Samoki. When he told the people there what to do, they did just as he said, and their jars were well shaped and beautiful. Then the Great Spirit saw that they were fit owners of the pottery, and he told them that they should always make many jars to sell.

In this way Lumawig taught the people and brought to them all the things which they now have.

Notes on this tale:

Lumawig is the greatest of all spirits and now lives in the sky, though for a time his home was in the Igorot village of Bontoc. He married a Bontoc girl, and the stones of their house are still to be seen in the village. It was Lumawig who created the Igorot, and ever since he has taken a great interest in them, teaching them how to overcome the forces of nature, how to plant, to reap and, in fact, everything that they know. Once each month a ceremony is held in his honor in a sacred grove, whose trees are believed to have sprung from the graves of his children. Here prayers are offered for health, good crops, and success in battle. A close resemblance exists between Lumawig of the Igorot and Kaboniyan of the Tinguian, the former being sometimes called Kambun'yan.

The Bukidnon of Mindanao have the following story: During a great drought Mampolompon could grow nothing on his clearing except one bamboo, and during a high wind this was broken. From this bamboo came a dog and a woman, who were the ancestors of the Moro.

At the north end of the village of Mayinit are a number of brackish hot springs, and from these the people secure the salt which has made the spot famous for miles around. Stones are placed in the shallow streams flowing from these springs, and when they have become encrusted with salt (about once a month) they are washed and the water is evaporated by boiling. The salt, which is then a thick paste, is formed into cakes and baked near the fire for about half an hour, when it is ready for use. It is the only salt in this section, and is in great demand. Even hostile tribes come to a hill overlooking the town and call down, then deposit whatever they have for trade and withdraw, while the Igorot take up the salt and leave it in place of the trade articles.

The women of Samoki are known as excellent potters, and their ware is used over a wide area. From a pit on a hillside to the north of the village they dig a reddish-brown clay, which they mix with a bluish mineral gathered on another hillside. When thoroughly mixed, this clay is placed on a board on the ground, and the potter, kneeling before it, begins her molding. Great patience and skill are required to bring the vessel to the desired shape. When it is completed it is set in the sun to dry for two or three days, after which it is ready for the baking. The new pots are piled tier above tier on the ground and blanketed with grass tied into bundles. Then pine bark is burned beneath and around the pile for about an hour, when the ware is sufficiently fired. It is then glazed with resin and is ready to market.

HOW THE MOON AND THE STARS CAME TO BE (BUKIDNON [MINDANAO])

One day in the times when the sky was close to the ground a spinster went out to pound rice. Before she began her work, she took off the beads from around her neck and the comb from her hair, and hung them on the sky, which at that time looked like coral rock.

Then she began working, and each time that she raised her pestle into the air it struck the sky. For some time she pounded the rice, and then she raised the pestle so high that it struck the sky very hard.

Immediately the sky began to rise, and it went up so far that she lost her ornaments. Never did they come down, for the comb became the moon and the beads are the stars that are scattered about.

Notes on this tale:
The common way to pound rice is to place a bundle of the grain on the ground on a dried carabao hide and pound it with a pestle to loosen the heads from the straw. When they are free they are poured into a mortar and again pounded with the pestle until the grain is separated from the chaff, after which it is winnowed.

According to the Klemantin myth (Borneo), the sky was raised when a giant named Usai accidentally struck it with his mallet while pounding rice.

ORIGIN (BAGOBO [MINDANAO])

In the beginning there lived one man and one woman, Toglai and Toglibon. Their first children were a boy and a girl. When they were old enough, the boy and the girl went far away across the waters seeking a good place to live in. Nothing more was heard of them until their children, the Spaniards and Americans, came back. After the first boy and girl left, other children were born to the couple; but they all remained at Cibolan on Mount Apo with their parents, until Toglai and Toglibon died and became spirits. Soon after that there came a great drought which lasted for three years. All the waters dried up, so that there were no rivers, and no plants could live.

"Surely," said the people, "Manama is punishing us, and we must go elsewhere to find food and a place to dwell in."

So they started out. Two went in the direction of the sunset, carrying with them stones from Cibolan River. After a long journey they reached a place where were broad fields of cogon grass and an abundance of water, and there they made their home. Their children still live in that place and are called Magindanau, because of the stones which the couple carried when they left Cibolan.

Two children of Toglai and Toglibon went to the south, seeking a home, and they carried with them women's baskets (baraan). When they found a good spot, they settled down. Their descendants, still dwelling at that place, are called Baraan or Bilaan, because of the women's baskets.

So two by two the children of the first couple left the land of their birth. In the place where each settled a new people developed, and thus it came about that all the tribes in the world received their names from things that the people carried out of Cibolan, or from the places where they settled.

All the children left Mount Apo save two (a boy and a girl), whom hunger and thirst had made too weak to travel. One day when they were about to die the boy crawled out to the field to see if there was one living thing, and to his surprise he found a stalk of sugarcane growing lustily. He eagerly cut it, and enough water came out to refresh him and his sister until the rains came. Because of this, their children are called Bagobo.

Note on the tale:
This is a good example of the way in which people at a certain stage try to account for their surroundings. Nearly all consider themselves the original people. We find the Bagobo no exception to this. In this tale, which is evidently very old, they account for themselves and their neighbors, and then, to meet present needs, they adapt the story to include the white people whom they have known for not more than two hundred years.

THE STORY OF THE CREATION (BILAAN [MINDANAO])

In the very beginning there lived a being so large that he cannot be compared with any known thing. His name was Melu, and when he sat on the clouds, which were his home, he occupied all the space above. His teeth were pure gold, and because he was very cleanly and continually rubbed himself with his hands, his skin became pure white. The dead skin which he rubbed off his body was placed on one side in a pile, and by and by this pile became so large that he was annoyed and set himself to consider what he could do with it.

Finally Melu decided to make the earth; so he worked very hard in putting the dead skin into shape, and when it was finished he was so pleased with it that he determined to make two beings like himself, though smaller, to live on it.

Taking the remnants of the material left after making the earth he fashioned two men, but just as they were all finished except their noses, Tau Tana from below the earth appeared and wanted to help him.

Melu did not wish any assistance, and a great argument ensued. Tau Tana finally won his point and made the noses which he placed on the people upside down. When all was finished, Melu and Tau Tana whipped the forms until they moved. Then Melu went to his home above the clouds, and Tau Tana returned to his place below the earth.

All went well until one day a great rain came, and the people on the earth nearly drowned from the water which ran off their heads into their noses. Melu, from his place on the clouds, saw their danger, and he came quickly to earth and saved their lives by turning their noses the other side up.

The people were very grateful to him, and promised to do anything he should ask of them. Before he left for the sky, they told him that they were very unhappy living on the great earth all alone, so he told them to save all the hair from their heads and the dry skin from their bodies and the next time he came he would make them some companions. And in this way there came to be a great many people on the earth.

Notes on this tale:

This story is well known among the Bilaan, who are one of the tribes least influenced by the Spaniards, and yet it bears so many incidents similar to biblical accounts that there is a strong suggestion of Christian influence. It is possible that these ideas came through the Mohammedan Moro.

Melu is the most powerful of the spirits and the one to whom the people resort in times of danger.

A similar story is found in British North Borneo.

IN THE BEGINNING (BILAAN [MINDANAO])

In the beginning there were four beings (Melu, Fiuweigh, Diwata, and Saweigh), and they lived on an island no larger than a hat. On this island there were no trees or grass or any other living thing besides these four people and one bird (Buswit). One day they sent this bird out across the waters to see what he could find, and when he returned he brought some earth, a piece of rattan, and some fruit.

Melu, the greatest of the four, took the soil and shaped it and beat it with a paddle in the same manner in which a woman shapes pots of clay, and when he finished he had made the earth. Then he planted the seeds from the fruit, and they grew until there was much rattan and many trees bearing fruit.

The four beings watched the growth for a long time and were well pleased with the work, but finally Melu said, "Of what use is this earth and all the rattan and fruit if there are no people?"

And the others replied, "Let us make some people out of wax."

So they took some wax and worked long, fashioning it into forms, but when they brought them to the fire the wax melted, and they saw that men could not be made in that way.

Next they decided to try to use dirt in making people, and Melu and one of his companions began working on that. All went well till they were ready to make the noses. The companion, who was working on that part, put them on upside down. Melu told him that the people would drown if he left them that way, but he refused to change them.

When his back was turned, however, Melu seized the noses, one by one, and turned them as they now are. But he was in such a hurry that he pressed his finger at the root, and it left a mark in the soft clay which you can still see on the faces of people.

THE CHILDREN OF THE LIMOKON (MANDAYA [MINDANAO])

In the very early days before there were any people on the earth, the limokon (a kind of dove) were very powerful and could talk like men though they looked like birds. One limokon laid two eggs, one at the mouth of the Mayo River and one farther up its course. After some time these eggs hatched, and the one at the mouth of the river became a man, while the other became a woman.

The man lived alone on the bank of the river for a long time, but he was very lonely and wished many times for a companion. One day when he was crossing the river something was swept against his legs with such force that it nearly caused him to drown. On examining it, he found that it was a hair, and he determined to go up the river and find whence it came. He traveled up the stream, looking on both banks, until finally he found the woman, and he was very happy to think that at last he could have a companion.

They were married and had many children, who are the Mandaya still living along the Mayo River.

Notes on this tale:

This origin story is of a very different type from those of the Bukidnon and Bagobo. While the others show foreign influence, this appears to be typically primitive.

The limokon is the omen bird of the Mandaya. It is believed to be a messenger from the spirit world which, by its calls, warns the people of danger or promises them success. If the coo of this bird comes from the right side, it is a good sign, but if it is on the left, in back, or in front, it is a bad sign, and the Mandaya knows that he must change his plans.

THE CREATION STORY (TAGALOG)

When the world first began there was no land, but only the sea and the sky, and between them was a kite (a bird something like a hawk). One day the bird which had nowhere to light grew tired of flying about, so she stirred up the sea until it threw its waters against the sky. The sky, in order to restrain the sea, showered upon it many islands until it could no longer rise, but ran back and forth. Then the sky ordered the kite to light on one of the islands to build her nest, and to leave the sea and the sky in peace.

Now at this time the land breeze and the sea breeze were married, and they had a child which was a bamboo. One day when this bamboo was floating about on the water, it struck the feet of the kite which was on the beach. The bird, angry that anything should strike it, pecked at the bamboo, and out of one section came a man and from the other a woman.

Then the earthquake called on all the birds and fish to see what should be done with these two, and it was decided that they should marry. Many children were born to the couple, and from them came all the different races of people.

After a while the parents grew very tired of having so many idle and useless children around, and they wished to be rid of them, but they knew of no place to send them to. Time went on and the children became so numerous that the parents enjoyed no peace. One day, in desperation, the father seized a stick and began beating them on all sides.

This so frightened the children that they fled in different directions, seeking hidden rooms in the house -- some concealed themselves in the walls, some ran outside, while others hid in the fireplace, and several fled to the sea.

Now it happened that those who went into the hidden rooms of the house later became the chiefs of the islands; and those who concealed themselves in the walls became slaves. Those who ran outside were free men; and those who hid in the fireplace became negroes; while those who fled to the sea were gone many years, and when their children came back they were the white people.

5 THE CREATION OF THE EARTH AND THE GREAT FLOOD (FROM GREEK AND ROMAN MYTHOLOGY)

Before there was earth or sea or heaven, there existed only chaos: shapeless, unorganized, lifeless matter. There was no sun, no moon, and no air. Elements existed, but they had neither form nor character. The earth was without firmness, the water without fluidity, and the sky without light.

There was opposition in all things: hot conflicted with cold, wet with dry, heavy with light, and hard with soft.

Finally a god, a natural higher force, resolved this conflict, separating earth from heaven, parting the dry land from the waters, and dividing the clear air from the clouds, thus organizing all things into a balanced union. In the highest sphere he made a heavenly vault of weightless and untainted ether. The next lower region he filled with air, light but not without substance. Then came the heavy earth, which sank down under its own weight and was encircled by the sea.

Thus did the god, whichever god it was, set order to the chaotic mass by separating it into its components, then organizing them into a harmonious whole.

Then the god shaped the earth into a great ball and caused the seas to spread in one direction and the other. He created springs, pools, and lakes, then formed rivers, causing them to flow toward the seas. He flattened out the plains, caused valleys to sink down, and pushed up mountains from the level places.

The earth he organized into five zones, the same number that exist in heaven, which is divided into two regions on the right, two on the left, and one in the center. On earth the middle zone is too hot for habitation and the two outer zones are too cold, but between these extremes the god created two temperate zones where heat and cold are balanced.

Beneath the ether and above the earth hangs the air, where the god formed mist and clouds, placing thunderbolts within the clouds. To each of the four winds he assigned limits and purpose. He caused the stars, which heretofore had been veiled in darkness, to shine forth across the sky.

The waters he filled with fishes, the earth with wild animals, and the air with birds. But none of these creatures approached the gods in intelligence; none could rightly be called master over all the others.

Then man was born. Either the god who had created this better earth made man from divine seed, or Prometheus, molded an image of the gods from a clump of earth that had been newly separated from the ether and thus still retained some divine qualities. Whoever created man, this new being was made to stand erect with his eyes directed toward heaven and the stars, unlike other animals who hang their heads and gaze toward the ground.

The first age of man was a golden age, during which men did what was right without laws and without the threat of punishment. No one strayed far from home. Everyone lived at peace with his neighbors, and the earth itself gave up its fruits without cultivation or labor. Berries, fruits, grains, and flowers abounded although the land remained untilled. Rivers flowed with milk and nectar, and honey dripped from the trees. Springtime was the only season.

When Saturn lost his rule to Jove this golden age on earth gave way to a silver age. Jove, the sky god, shortened springtime and added the seasons of summer, fall, and winter. The earth now yielded its bounty of grain only from plowed fields, made fruitful by the labor of man and beast.

Then came an age of bronze. Just as bronze is harder than silver, men were now more disposed toward warfare than heretofore.

Finally came an age of iron, a metal baser and harder than gold, silver, or bronze. Now the natural virtues of man gave way to baser, harsher qualities. Modesty, truth, and loyalty were replaced by treachery, deceit, and greed. Sailors now traversed the seas seeking new lands and power. Men sought wealth in foreign places and from beneath the earth, wealth that in turn became the cause of much wickedness and suffering. Friend betrayed friend, and relative turned against relative.

The conflict on earth threatened even heaven. Legends tell how at that time giants attempted an attack on the realm of the gods by piling mountains together to reach the sky. Jove defended his heavenly kingdom with a mighty thunderbolt, which destroyed the tower of mountains, crushing the giants beneath it as it fell. Torrents of blood flowed forth from their bodies, drenching the earth. It is said that from this blood-soaked earth was born a new breed of men, who like their giant forebears had no respect for the gods.

Looking down from his kingdom in the sky, Jove saw that mankind was now hopelessly violent and cruel. He called together his council, and they came to him forthwith, traveling that famous bright path across heaven's vault, the Milky Way. Jove angrily demanded that the utterly corrupt human race be destroyed, promising that afterward he himself would supervise the creation of a new stock of men. The gods sadly agreed that only this extreme act would solve the threat of mankind's wickedness.

Jove was about to strike the earth with a barrage of thunderbolts when he realized that the conflagration caused by such an attack might threaten heaven itself, so he resolved to destroy the earth's inhabitants by water instead of by fiery lightning. To this end he fettered the North Wind, then charged the South Wind to bring forth endless rains. Jove's brother Neptune, god of the seas, caused the tides and the waves to rise upon the land and the rivers to overflow their banks.

Man and beast alike fell prey to the ever-rising flood. Orchards and planted fields were washed away. Houses and other buildings were either demolished by the crashing waves or submerged beneath a sea that had no shores. Not even the temples and sacred images were spared. The birds themselves, their wings finally tiring from continuous flight, in the end were forced to surrender to watery graves.

In the end only one place on earth remained above water: the twin summits of Mount Parnassus. It was here that the small boat carrying Deucalion and his wife Pyrrha ran aground. They alone had survived the great deluge.

When Jove saw that only one man and one woman were still alive on earth, and that this husband and this wife were virtuous people, both true worshippers, he released the North Wind and caused it to dissipate the storms and clouds. Then Neptune called upon Triton to recall the tides and waves with a signal from his conch-shell trumpet.

The earth was now restored, but lifeless, desolate, and empty. Deucalion and Pyrrha, seeing that they were the only living beings left on earth, sought guidance by going together to the Waters of Cephissus, which were again flowing in their usual channel. They sprinkled themselves with this holy water, then entered the temple and asked for assistance. The answer came through an oracle that they should leave the temple and scatter behind them their mothers' bones.

Deucalion could not believe his ears, and Pyrrha stated aloud that she would never dishonor her mother's spirit by thus disturbing her bones. Deucalion, however, thought that the words of the oracle were not to be taken literally, that the mother mentioned was not a human mother, but rather mother earth, and that the bones to be scattered were stones from the earth's body. Deciding to put this interpretation to the test, Deucalion and Pyrrha scattered behind them stones from the earth.

No one would believe what happened afterward, if it were not for the testimony of ancient legends. The stones, once thrown to the ground, lost their hardness and assumed human forms. Those scattered by Deucalion became male, and those scattered by Pyrrha became female. And thus the earth was repopulated.

Then through the natural process of warmth and moisture and earth reacting with one another the lower animals were reborn as well. Yes, fire and water are opposites, but moist heat is the source of all living things. Creation comes about through the resolution of opposing forces.

6 KABYL CREATION AND ORIGIN MYTHS

(The Kabyl people belong to the Berbers of North Africa. They are native to the Djurdjura Mountains of Algeria.)

THE FIRST HUMAN BEINGS

In the beginning there were only one man and one woman and they lived not on the earth but beneath it. They were the first people in the world and neither knew that the other was of another sex.

One day they both came to the well to drink. The man said, "Let me drink."

The woman said, "No, I'll drink first. I was here first."

The man tried to push the woman aside. She struck him. They fought. The man smote the woman so that she dropped to the ground. Her clothing fell to one side. Her thighs were naked.

The man saw the woman lying strange and naked before him. He saw that she had a taschunt. He felt that he had a thabuscht. He looked at the taschunt and asked, "What is that for?"

The woman said, "That is good."

The man lay upon the woman. He lay with the woman eight days.

After nine months the woman bore four daughters. Again, after nine months, she bore four sons, And again four daughters and again four sons. So at last the man and the woman had fifty daughters and fifty sons. The father and the mother did not know what to do with so many children. So they sent them away.

The fifty maidens went off together towards the north. The fifty young men went off together towards the east. After the maidens had been on their way northwards under the earth for a year, they saw a light above them. There was a hole in the earth.

The maidens saw the sky above them and cried, "Why stay under the earth when we can climb to the surface where we can see the sky?"

The maidens climbed up through the hole and on to the earth.

The fifty youths likewise continued in their own direction under the earth for a year until they, too, came to a place where there was a hole in the crust and they could see the sky above them.

The youths looked at the sky and cried, "Why remain under the earth when there is a place from which one can see the sky?"

So they climbed through their hole to the surface.

Thereafter the fifty maidens went their way over the earth's surface and the youths went their way and none knew aught of the others.

At that time all trees and plants and stones could speak. The fifty maidens saw the plants and asked them, "Who made you?"

And the plants replied, "The earth."

The maidens asked the earth, "Who made you?"

And the earth replied, "I was already here."

During the night the maidens saw the moon and the stars and they cried, "Who made you that you stand so high over us and over the trees? Is it you who give us light? Who are you, great and little stars? Who created you? Or are you, perhaps, the ones who have made everything else?" All the maidens called and shouted. But the moon and the stars were so high that they could not answer.

The youths had wandered into the same region and could hear the fifty maidens shouting.

They said to one another, "Surely here are other people like ourselves. Let us go and see who they are." And they set off in the direction from which the shouts had come.

But just before they reached the place they came to the bank of a great stream. The stream lay between the fifty maidens and the fifty youths. The youths had, however, never seen a river before, so they shouted. The maidens heard the shouting in the distance and came towards it.

The maidens reached the other bank of the river, saw the fifty youths and cried, "Who are you? What are you shouting? Are you human beings, too?"

The fifty youths shouted back, "We, too, are human beings. We have come out of the earth. But what are you yelling about?"

The maidens replied, "We, too, are human beings and we, too, have come out of the earth. We shouted and asked the moon and the stars who had made them or if they had made everything else."

The fifty boys spoke to the river, "You are not like us," they said. "We cannot grasp you and cannot pass over you as one can pass over the earth. What are you? How can one cross over you to the other side?"

The river said, "I am the water. I am for bathing and washing. I am there to drink. If you want to reach my other shore go upstream to the shallows. There you can cross over me."

The fifty youths went upstream, found the shallows and crossed over to the other shore. The fifty youths now wished to join the fifty maidens, but the latter cried, "Do not come too close to us. We won't stand for it. You go over there, and we'll stay here leaving that strip of steppe between us."

So the fifty youths and the fifty maidens continued on their way, some distance, apart, but traveling in the same direction.

One day the fifty boys came to a spring. The fifty maidens also came to a spring.

The youths said, "Did not the river tell us that water was to bathe in? Come, let us bathe."

The fifty youths laid aside their clothing and stepped down into the water and bathed. The fifty maidens sat around their spring and saw the youths in the distance. A bold maiden said, "Come with me and we shall see what the other human beings are doing."

Two maidens replied, "We'll come with you." All the others refused.

The three maidens crept through the bushes towards the fifty youths. Two of them stopped on the way. Only the bold maiden came, hidden by the bushes, to the very place where the youths were bathing. Through the bushes the maiden looked at the youths who had laid aside their clothing. The youths were naked. The maiden looked at all of them. She saw that they were not like the maidens. She looked at everything carefully. As the youths dressed again the maiden crept away without their having seen her.

The maiden returned to the other maidens who gathered around her and asked, "What have you seen?"

The bold maiden replied, "Come, we'll bathe, too, and then I can tell you and show you."

The fifty maidens undressed and stepped down into their spring.

The bold maiden told them, "The people over there are not as we are. Where our breasts are, they have nothing. Where our taschunt is, they have something else. The hair on their heads is not long like ours, but short. And when one sees them naked one's heart pounds and one wishes to embrace them. When one has seen them naked, one can never forget it."

The other maidens replied, "You lie."

But the bold maiden said, "Go and see for yourselves and you'll come back feeling as I do."

The other maidens replied, "We'll continue on our way."

The fifty maidens continued on their way and so did the fifty youths. But the youths went ahead slowly. The maidens, on the other hand, described a half circle so that they crossed the path of the youths. They camped quite close to one another.

On this day the youths said, "Let us not sleep under the sky any more. Let us build houses."

A few of the youths began to make themselves holes in the earth. They slept in the holes. Others made themselves passages and rooms under the earth and slept in them. But a few of the youths said, "What are you doing digging into the earth to make houses? Are there not stones here that we can pile them one upon the other?"

The youths gathered stones and piled them one on the other in layers. When they had built the walls one of them went off and began to fell a tree.

But the tree cried and said, "What, you will cut me down? What are you doing? Do you think you are older than I? What do you think to gain by it?"

The youth answered, "I am not older than you, nor do I wish to be presumptuous. I simply wish to cut down fifty of you trees and lay the trunks across my house for a roof. Your branches and twigs I will lay within the house to protect them from the wet."

The tree answered, "That is well."

The youth then cut down fifty trees, laid their trunks across his house and covered them with earth. The branches he cut up and stored away inside the house. A few of the larger trunks he set upright in the house to carry the weight of the roof. When the others saw how fine the house was they did even as he had done.

Among the youths there was a wild one, just as among the maidens one was wild and untamed. This wild youth would not live in a house. Rather he preferred to creep in and out among the houses of the others seeking someone whom he could rend and devour. For he was so wild that he thought only of killing and eating others.

The fifty maidens were encamped at a distance. Looking, they saw how the fifty youths first dug themselves holes and tunnels in the earth and how they finally built their houses.

They asked one another, "What are these other humans doing? What are they doing with the stones and the trees?"

The bold maiden said, "I'll go there again. I will sneak over and see what these other humans are doing. I have seen them naked once and I want to see them again."

The bold maiden crawled through the bushes to the houses. She came quite close. Finally she slid into a house. There was no one there. The maiden looked around and saw how fine the house was. The wild one came by outside. He scented the maiden. He roared. The maiden screamed and, dashing out of the house, made for the place where the other maidens were encamped.

All the youths heard the maiden scream and all jumped up and ran after her. The maiden ran through the bushes and screamed. The other maidens heard her. They sprang to their feet and ran in her direction to help her. In the bushes the fifty maidens and the fifty youths came together, each maiden with a youth.

They fought in the bushes, the maidens with the youths. Even the wild maiden encountered the wild youth in the bushes.

It was dark in the bushes and they fought in pairs. No pair could see the next one. The fifty maidens were strong. They hurled the fifty youths to the ground, and threw themselves on top of them. And they said to themselves, "Now I will see at last if the bold maiden lied."

The maidens seized the youths between the thighs. They found the thabuscht. As they touched it, it swelled and the youths lay quite still. As the maidens felt the thabuscht of the youths, their hearts began to swell. The fifty maidens threw aside their clothes and inserted the thabuscht in their taschunt. The youths lay quite still. The fifty maidens began to ravish the fifty youths. Thereupon the fifty youths became more active than the fifty maidens.

Every youth took a maiden and brought her into his house. They married.

In the house the youths said, "It is not right that the woman lies on the man. In the future we shall see to it that the man lies on the woman. In this way we will become your masters." And in the future they slept in the fashion customary among the Kabyls today.

The youths were now much more active than the maidens, and all lived happily together in great satisfaction. Only the wild youth and the wild maiden, who had no house, roamed here and there seeking others to devour. The others chased them, and when they met them they beat them.

The wild ones said to each other, "We must be different from these humans that they treat us so badly. We will do better to keep out of their way. Let us leave this place and go to the forest."

The wild ones left and went to the forest from which, in future, they emerged only to steal children whom they devoured. The wild maiden became the first teriel (witch) and the wild youth the first lion. And they both lived on human flesh. The other young men and women were happy to be rid of the cannibals. They lived happily with one another. Their food consisted only of plants, which they uprooted.

THE BEGINNING OF AGRICULTURE

Meanwhile the first man and the first woman wandered under the earth. One day they found a great pile of millet in a corner. Beside it lay piles of barley and wheat and seeds of all the food plants. A pile of everything lay in a corner.

The first man and the first woman looked at the seeds and asked, "What does this mean?"

An ant was running along beside the piles of seeds. The first man and the first woman saw the ant. The ant removed a grain of wheat from its husk. The ant ate the grain of wheat.

The first man asked, "What is the ant doing?"

The woman said, "Kill it! Kill the ugly creature!"

The man said, "Why should I kill it? Someone created it just as someone created us."

The man did nothing to the ant but watched it instead.

The first man asked the ant, "Tell me what you are doing. Can you tell me anything about the millet and the barley and these other seeds?"

The ant said, "I will ask you something. Do you know of a spring, of a brook or of a river?"

The first man said, "No, we know only the well."

The ant said, "Then you know what water is. The water is there so that one may wash one's self and one's clothing. The water is there that one may drink. It is also there that one may cook one's food. All this grain is good if one cooks it in water. Now come with me. I will show you and the first woman everything."

The first man said, "We will come with you."

The ant led the first parents to its hole which led from under the earth to the earth's surface.

The ant said, "This is my path, come on my path with me."

The ant led the first parents through the passageway and on up to the surface. The ant led them to a river and said, "Here flows the water in which you may wash yourselves and your clothing and which you may drink. This is the water with which you cook your corn after you have ground it."

The ant led the first parents to some stones and said, "These are the stones with which you grind the corn to meal."

The ant showed them how to lay one stone on the other and how to insert a stick in order to turn the upper stone. The ant showed them how the grain should lie between the two stones. The ant said to the first parents, "This is a house-mill. With it you must grind the grain to meal." The ant helped the first human beings to grind the corn.

The ant showed the first woman how to make dough with water and meal and how to knead it. The ant said to the first woman, "Now you must make a fire." The ant took two stones from the river bed and took some dried plants and said, "This is a fire tool." The ant also brought dried grass and wood.

The ant struck a fire with the flint and threw wood and twigs on it.

The ant said to the first woman, "When the fire has grown strong and large and has become a heap of glowing ashes you must clear it to one side. On the hot place you must lay your flat cakes of kneaded dough. Then cover them up and throw the hot ashes and the glowing coals over them. After a while the bread will be cooked and you will be able to eat it."

The first woman did what the ant had told her. And when she had cleared away the ashes for the second time the bread was done. The first man and the first woman ate the bread and said, "Now we have full stomachs."

The first man said to the woman, "Come, we will take a look at the earth."

The first man and the first woman took plenty of barley and wheat with them, and they took the millstones with them and they wandered over the earth. On the way they lost, here and there, a few grains of wheat and barley. Rain fell. The grain which had fallen to the ground took root, grew and bore fruit. The first parents came to the place where the forty-nine young men had built houses and where they lived with the forty-nine maidens as their wives. Till then the forty-nine young men and the forty-nine maidens had eaten only plants which they plucked from the earth. The first parents showed them how to make bread even as they had learned it from the ant. The forty-nine young men and women ate their first bread.

They told their parents, "This food is very good. We would like to accompany you to the place where you found the ant and the grain in order to fetch some more of it."

The first parents went back with the forty-nine young men and their wives.

On the way back they saw the wheat and barley which had sprung up out of the grain which they had lost and which had fallen to the ground.

They said, "That is the same grain which the ant showed us how to cook and eat." They grubbed up the earth and found that each plant had grown up out of a single grain.

They said, "Every grain which fell to the earth has brought forth twenty to thirty grains. In future we will eat half our grain and put the other half in the earth."

They threw half of their grain on the earth. But it was the dry season and the sun burned. The corn didn't grow. They waited and waited but the corn did not appear.

Thereupon, they went to the ant and said, "When we let a few grains fall for the first time they took root and grew and each grain produced twenty and thirty others. Now we have thrown grain on to the earth again, and not a single stalk has appeared. What is the reason?"

The ant answered, "You have not chosen the right season. After it has been hot for a long time you must wait till rain has fallen. When the earth is damp then throw in your corn. And then it will rain again and you will enjoy a rich harvest. But if you throw your grain on the earth in the hot season it will bum up and you will harvest nothing, for the grain will have been dried up."

And the human beings said, "Aha, so one must do it that way!"

Men thereafter did as the ant had taught them. They sowed half their grain after the first rains had fallen. The grain waxed and each stalk bore twenty-fold and thirty-fold. And the other half of their grain they ate.

7 THE CREATION OF LIFE ON EARTH: A MODERN DAY CREATION STORY (FROM THE RAELIAN MOVEMENT)

Scientists from another planet created all life on earth using DNA.

On December 13, 1973, in the heart of the Puy de Lassolas crater, near Clermond-Ferrand in the center of France, a journalist, Claude Vorilhon, saw a metallic looking engine about 7 meters in diameter in the shape of a flattened bell descend from the sky. It resembled no existing terrestrial technology.

Astounded, he saw the engine stop and a trap door open. A human being of small size (1.2 meters) descended and approached him. Reassured by the pacifist attitude of the visitor, Claude Vorilhon wanted to communicate, and questioned him in French, "Where do you come from?"

He heard the small being answer, "From very far, from another planet. I have come to meet you, you Claude Vorilhon. I have many things to tell you, and I have chosen you for a difficult mission. You are going to transmit to humans what I am going to tell you, and according to their reactions we will see if we can officially show ourselves to them. I know that you have recently read the Bible. Come into my machine. We will be more comfortable to talk."

The extra-terrestrial was about four feet in height, had long dark hair, almond-shaped eyes, olive skin, and exuded harmony and humor. He gave Claude Vorilhon the name Rael, then told him, "We were the ones who made all life on earth. You mistook us for gods. We were at the origin of your main religions. Now that you are mature enough to understand this, we would like to enter official contact through an embassy."

The messages dictated to Rael explain how life on Earth is not the result of random evolution, nor the work of a supernatural "God." It is a deliberate creation, using DNA, by a scientifically advanced people who made human beings literally in their image, what one can call "scientific creationism."

References to these scientists and their work, as well as to their symbol of infinity can be found in the ancient texts of many cultures. For example, in Genesis, the biblical account of creation, the word "Elohim" has been mistranslated as "God" in the singular, but it is a plural, which means "those who came from the sky."

A very long time ago on a distant planet, the development of knowledge made it possible to scientifically create life. The ethics committees at the time, which were put in place by this distant government, banned such experiments from being done on their planet.

The scientific teams were given the material and technological means to go and explore other planets in order to continue these projects deemed dangerous for the population.

Our planet, "the Earth," was one of these sites where such research was applied, in particular the synthesis of life in laboratories.

They made reconnaissance flights, and artificial satellites were placed around the Earth to study its constitution and atmosphere, as we are currently doing on Mars or Jupiter.

Then, they started a vast terraforming project, in other words, planning of the soil and the implementation of a big colony of technicians, scientists in all disciplines, and artists. They pursued the project they were forced to stop on their planet of origin: the creation of life.

The work done in genetic engineering allowed them to conceive all imaginable life forms on a planet which could offer such a luxury of possibilities, since it was virgin.

After the creation of elementary life forms from the synthesis of DNA, they created more complex forms. First was plant life. Then there were the aquatic animals, which were carefully conceived so as to find the right ecological balance. Then came birds of all sorts. The conjunction of the scientist's and artist's ideas gave diverse and remarkable colors, forms, and attitudes to life on earth.

Despite strict directives from their government, after the creation of terrestrial animals some scientists were tempted to reproduce a being with human shape and behavior. These works, which were done in total secrecy, succeeded after a long period of trials and prototypes. The public opinion on their planet was scandalized when they discovered the facts. Public opinion was forced to accept that the first humans were a reality. So, the experiment was continued officially, with orders as strict as the previous ones: to keep these new creatures in total ignorance of their origin.

At this time in their history, these scientists were not aware yet that they had given birth to a new humanity on earth, our humanity. They were merely repeating an unwavering cycle in the cosmos: The created will one day become creator.

8 HOW THE WORLD BEGAN (A SENECA CREATION MYTH)

Beyond the dome we call the sky there is another world. There in the most ancient of times was a fair country where lived the great chief of the up-above-world and his people, the celestial beings. This chief had a wife who was very aged in body, having survived many seasons.

In that upper world there were many things of which men of today know nothing. This world floated like a great cloud and journeyed where the great chief wished it to go. The crust of that world was not thick, but none of these men beings knew what was under the crust.

In the center of that world there grew a great tree which bore flowers and fruits, and all the people lived from the fruits of the tree and were satisfied. Now, moreover, the tree bore a great blossom at its top, and it was luminous and lighted the world above, and wonderful perfume filled the air which the people breathed. The rarest perfume of all was that which resembled the smoke of sacred tobacco, and this was the incense greatly loved by the great chief. It grew from the leaves that sprouted from the roots of the tree.

The roots of the tree were white and ran in four directions. Far through the earth they ran, giving firm support to the tree. Around this tree the people gathered daily, for here the Great Chief had his lodge where he dwelt. Now, in a dream he was given a desire to take as his wife a certain maiden who was very fair to look upon.

(*Footnote by Arthur C. Parker: In another version this chief was killed and his body hidden In the trunk of the celestial tree. Another chief, a rival, desired to marry the daughter of the deceased one and indeed took her in the manner here related. In this version it was the bride who desired to have the tree uprooted in order that she might hunt for her father's body. The concealing of the body of the celestial father in the body of a tree reminds one of the legend of Osiris.)

So, he took her as his wife for when he had embraced her he found her most pleasing. When he had eaten the marriage bread he took her to his lodge, and to his surprise found that she was with child. This caused him great anger and he felt himself deceived, but the woman loved the child, which had been conceived by the potent breath of her lover when he had embraced her. He was greatly distressed, for this fair Awen'ha'i was of the noblest family. It is she who is customarily called Iagen'tci.

He, the Ancient One, fell into a troubled sleep and a dream commanded him to have the celestial tree uprooted as a punishment to his wife, and as a relief of his troubled spirit. So on the morrow he announced to his wife that he had a dream and could not be satisfied until it had been divined. Thereupon she "discovered his word," and it was that the tree should be uprooted.

"Truly you have spoken," said Ancient One, "and now my mind shall be satisfied."

And the woman, his wife, saw that there was trouble ahead for the sky world, but she too found pleasure in the uprooting of the tree, wishing to know what was beneath it. Yet did she know that to uproot the tree meant disaster for her, through the anger of Ancient One against her.

It so happened that the chief called all his people together and they endeavored to uproot the tree, it being deep-rooted and firm. Then did the chief grow even more angry for Iagen'tci had cried out that calamity threatened and nobody would avert it. Then did the chief himself embrace the tree and with a mighty effort uprooted it, throwing it far away. His effort was tremendous, and in uprooting the tree he shook down fruits and leaves. Thereafter he went into his lodge and entered into the apartment where his wife Iagen'tci lay moaning that she too must be satisfied by a look into the hole. So the chief led her to the hole made by uprooting the tree.

He caused her to seat herself on the edge of the hole and peer downward. Again his anger returned against her, for she said nothing to indicate that she had been satisfied. Long she sat looking into the hole until the chief in rage drew her blanket over her head and pushed her with his foot, seeking to thrust her into the hole, and be rid of her.

As he did this she grasped the earth at her side and gathered in her fingers all manner of seeds that had fallen from the shaken tree. In her right hand she held the leaves of the plant that smelled like burning tobacco, for it grew from a root that had been broken off. Again the chief pushed the woman, whose curiosity had caused the destruction of the greatest blessing of the up-above-world. It was a mighty push, and despite her hold upon the plant and upon the ground, she fell into the hole.

Now, this hole had penetrated the crust of the upper world, and when Iagen'tci fell she went far down out of sight, and the chief could not see her in the depths of the darkness below. As she fell she beheld a beast that emitted fire from its head whom she called Gaas'iondie't'ha (Gahashondietoh).

It is said that as she passed by him he took out a small pot, a corn mortar, a pestle, a marrow bone, and an ear of corn and presented them to her, saying, "Because thou hast thus done, thou shalt eat by these things, for there is nothing below, and all who eat shall see me once, and it will be the last."

Now it is difficult to know how this Fire Beast can be seen, for he is of the color of the wind and is of the color of anything that surrounds it, though some say be is pure white.

Hovering over the troubled waters below were other creatures, some like and some unlike those that were created afterward. It is said by the old people that in those times lived the spirit of Ga'ha' and of S'hagodiiowen'gowa, of Hi'non' and of Deiodasondaiko (the Wind, the Defending Face, the Thunder, and the Heavy Night). There were also what seemed to be ducks upon the water and these also saw the descending figure.

The creature-beings knew that a new body was coming to them and that here below there was no abiding place for her. They took council together and sought to devise a way to provide for her.

It was agreed that the duck-creatures should receive her on their interknit wings and lower her gently to the surface below. The great turtle from the underworld was to arise and make his broad back a resting place. It was as has been agreed, and the woman came down upon the floating island.

Then did the creatures seek to make a world for the woman, and one by one they dove to the bottom of the water seeking to find earth to plant upon the turtle's back. A duck dived but went so far that it breathed the water and came up dead. A pickerel went down and came back dead. Many creatures sought to find the bottom of the water but could not.

At last the creature called Muskrat made the attempt and only succeeded in touching the bottom with his nose, but this was sufficient for he was enabled to smear it upon the shell and the earth immediately grew, and as the earth-substance increased so did the size of the turtle.

After a time the woman, who lay prone, aroused herself and released what was in her hands, dropping many seeds into the folds of her garment. Likewise she spread out the earth from the heaven world which she had grasped and thus caused the seeds to spring into germination as they dropped from her dress.

The root of the tree which she had grasped sunk into the soil where she had fallen and this too began to grow until it formed a tree with all manner of fruits and flowers and bore a luminous orb at its top by which the new world became illuminated.

Now in due season the Sky-Woman lay beneath the tree and to her a daughter was born. She was then happy, for she had a companion. Rapidly the girl child grew until very soon she could run about.

It was then the custom of Ancient One to say: "My daughter, run about the island and return telling me what you have seen."

Day by day the girl ran around the island, and each time it became larger, making her trips longer and longer. She observed that the earth was carpeted with grass and that shrubs and trees were springing up everywhere. This she reported to her mother, who sat beneath the centrally situated great tree.

In one part of the island there was a tree on which grew a long vine, and upon this vine the girl was accustomed to swing for amusement, and her body moved to and fro giving her great delight.

Then did her mother say, "My daughter, you laugh as if being embraced by a lover. Have you seen a man?"

"I have seen no one but you, my mother," answered the girl, "but when I swing I know someone is close to me, and I feel my body embraced as if with strong arms. I feel thrilled, and I tingle, which causes me to laugh."

Then did the Sky-Woman look sad, and she said, "My daughter, I know not now what will befall us. You are married to Ga'ha', and he will be the father of your children. There will be two boys."

In due season the voices of two boys were heard speaking, eia'da'gon', and the words of one were kind, and he gave no trouble, but the words of the other were harsh, and he desired to kill his mother. His skin was covered with warts and boils, and he was inclined to cause great pain.

When the two boys were born Elder One made his mother happy, but when Warty One was born he pierced her through the armpit and stood upon her dead body. So did the mother perish, and because of this the Sky-Woman wept.

The boys required little care but instantly became able to care for themselves. After the mother's body bad been arranged for burial, the Sky-Woman saw the Elder One whom she called Good-Mind, approach, and he said, "Grandmother, I wish to help you prepare the grave." So he helped his grandmother who continually wept, and deposited the body of his mother in a grave.

Thereupon did the grandmother speak to her daughter, "Oh, my daughter," she said, "you have departed and made the first path to the world from which I came bringing your life. When you reach that homeland make ready to receive many beings from this place below, for I think the path will be trodden by many." Good-Mind watched at the grave of his mother and watered the earth above it until the grass grew. He continued to watch until he saw strange buds coming out of the ground.

Where the feet were the earth sprouted with a plant that became the stringed-potato, where her fingers lay sprang the beans, where her abdomen lay sprang the squash, where her breasts lay sprang the corn plant, and from the spot above her forehead sprang the tobacco plant.

Now the warty one was named Evil-Mind, and he neglected his mother's grave and spent his time tearing up the land and seeking to do evil.

When the grandmother saw the plants springing from the grave of her daughter and cared for by Good-Mind she was thankful and said, "By these things we shall hereafter live, and they shall be cooked in pots with fire, and the corn shall be your milk and sustain you. You shall make the corn grow in hills like breasts, for from the corn shall flow our living."

Then the grandmother, the Sky-Woman, took Good-Mind about the island and instructed him how to produce plants and trees. So he spoke to the earth and said, "Let a willow here come forth," and it came. In a like manner he made the oak, the chestnut, the beech, the hemlock, the spruce, the pine, the maple, the buttonball, the tulip, the elm, and many other trees that should become useful.

With a jealous stomach the Evil-Mind followed behind and sought to destroy the good things but could not, so he spoke to the earth and said, "Briars come forth," and they came forth. Likewise he created poisonous plants and thorns upon bushes.

Upon a certain occasion Good-Mind made inquiries of his grandmother, asking where his father dwelt.

Then did the Sky-Woman say, "You shall now seek your father. He lives to the uttermost east, and you shall go to the far eastern end of the island and go over the water until you behold a mountain rising from the sea. You shall walk up the mountain, and there you will find your father seated upon the top."

Good-Mind made the pilgrimage and came to the mountain.

At the foot of the mountain he looked upward and called, "My father, where art thou?"

And a great voice sounded the word, "A son of mine shall cast the cliff from the mountain's edge to the summit of this peak."

Good-Mind grasped the cliff and with a mighty effort flung it to the mountaintop.

Again he cried, "My father, where art thou?"

The answer came, "A son of mine shall swim the cataract from the pool below to the top."

Good-Mind leaped into the falls and swam upward to the top where the water poured over.

He stood there and cried again, "My father, where art thou?"

The voice answered, "A son of mine shall wrestle with the wind."

So, there at the edge of a terrifying precipice Good-Mind grappled with Wind, and the two wrestled, each endeavoring to throw the other over. It was a terrible battle and Wind tore great rocks from the mountainside and lashed the water below, but Good-Mind overcame Wind, and he departed moaning in defeat.

Once more Good-Mind called, "My father, where art thou?"

In awesome tones the voice replied, "A son of mine shall endure the flame," and immediately a flame sprang out of the mountain side and enveloped Good-Mind. It blinded him and tortured him with its cruel heat, but he threw aside its entwining arms and ran to the mountain top where he beheld a being sitting in the midst of a blaze of light.

"I am thy father," said the voice. "Thou art my son."

"I have come to receive power," said the son. "I wish to rule all things on the earth."

"You have power," answered the father. "You have conquered. I give to you the bags of life, the containers of living creatures that will bless the earth."

Thus did the father and son counsel together, and the son learned many things that he should do. He learned how to avoid the attractive path that descended to the place of the cave where Hanishe'onoln' dwells.

Now the father said, "How did you come to find me, seeing I am secluded by many elements?"

The Good-Mind answered, "When I was about to start my journey Sky-Woman, my grandmother, gave me a flute, and I blew upon it, making music. Now, when the music ceased the flute spoke to me, saying, 'This way shalt thou go,' and I continued to make music, and the voice of the flute spoke to me."

Then did the father say, "Make music by the flute and listen, then shalt thou continue to know the right direction."

In course of time Good-Mind went down the mountain and he waded the sea, taking with him the bags with which he had been presented. As he drew near the shore he became curious to know what was within, and he pinched one bag hoping to feel its contents. He felt a movement inside, which increased until it became violent. The bag began to roll about on his back until he could scarcely hold it, and a portion of the mouth of the bag slipped from his hand.

Immediately the things inside began to jump out and fall into the water with a great splash, and they were water animals of different kinds. The other bag began to roll around on his back, but he held on very tight, but it slipped and fell into the water, and many kinds of swimming creatures rushed forth, fishes, crabs and eels.

The fourth bag then began to roll about, but he held on until he reached the land when he threw it down, and out rushed all the good land animals, of kinds he did not know. From the bird bag had come good insects, and from the fish bag had also come little turtles and clams.

When Good-Mind came to his grandmother beneath the tree she asked what he had brought, for she heard music in the trees and saw creatures scampering about. Thereupon Good-Mind related what had happened, and Sky-Woman said, "We must now call all the animals and discover their names, and moreover we must so treat them that they will have fat."

So then she spoke, "Cavity be in the ground and be filled with oil." The pool of oil came, for Sky-Woman had the power of creating what she desired.

Good-Mind then caught the animals one by one and brought them to his grandmother. She took a large furry animal and cast it into the pool and it swam very slowly across, licking up much oil. "This animal shall hereafter be known as bear, and you shall be very fat."

Next came another animal with much fur, and it swam across and licked up the oil, and it was named buffalo. So in turn were named the elk, the moose, the badger, the woodchuck, and the raccoon, and all received much fat. Then came the bealking about. He walked over to the place where the being was pacing to and fro. He saw that it was S'hagodiiwen'gowa, who was a giant with a grotesque face.

"I am master of the earth," roared this being (called also Great Defender), for he was the whirlwind.

"If you are master," said Good-Mind, "prove your power."

Defender said, "What shall be our test?"

"Let this be the test," said Good-Mind, "that the mountain yonder shall approach us at your bidding."

So Defender spoke saying, "Mountain, come hither." And they turned their backs that they might not see it coming until it stood at their backs. Soon they turned about again, and the mountain had not moved.

"So now I shall command," said Good-Mind, and he spoke saying, "Mountain, come hither," and they turned their backs. There was a rushing of air, and Defender turned to see what was behind him and fell against the onrushing mountain, and it bent his nose and twisted his mouth, and from this he never recovered.

Then did Defender say, "I do now acknowledge you to be master. Command me and I will obey."

"Since you love to wander," said Good-Mind, "it shall be your duty to move about over the earth and stir up things. You shall abandon your evil intentions and seek to overcome your otgont nature, changing it to be of benefit to man-beings, whom I am about to create."

"Then," said Defender, "shall man-beings offer ince lived.

When he saw them he said unto them, "All this world I give unto you. It is from me that you shall say you are descended and you are the children of the firstborn of earth, and you shall say that you are the flesh of Iagen'tci, she the Ancient-Bodied-One.

When he had acquainted them with the other first beings, and shown them how to hunt and fish and to eat of the fruits of the land, he told them that they should seek to live together as friends and brothers and that they should treat each other well.

He told them how to give incense of tobacco, for Awen'ha'i', Ancient-Bodied-One, had stripped the heaven world of tobacco when she fell, and thus its incense should be a pleasing one into which men-beings might speak their words when addressing him hereafter. These and many other things did he tell them.

Soon he vanished from the sight of created men beings, and he took all the first beings with him upon the sky road.

Soon men-beings began to increase, and they covered the earth, and from them we are descended. Many things have happened since those days, so much that all can never be told.

9 THE CREATION OF HEAVEN AND EARTH (ACCORDING TO THE FIRST BOOK OF MOSES CALLED GENESIS, KING JAMES VERSION)

CHAPTER 1

In the beginning God created the heaven and the earth.

And the earth was without form, and void; and darkness was upon the face of the deep. And the Spirit of God moved upon the face of the waters.

And God said, Let there be light: and there was light.

And God saw the light, that it was good: and God divided the light from the darkness.

And God called the light Day, and the darkness he called Night. And the evening and the morning were the first day.

And God said, Let there be a firmament in the midst of the waters, and let it divide the waters from the waters.

And God made the firmament, and divided the waters which were under the firmament from the waters which were above the firmament: and it was so.

And God called the firmament Heaven. And the evening and the morning were the second day.

And God said, Let the waters under the heaven be gathered together unto one place, and let the dry land appear: and it was so.

And God called the dry land Earth; and the gathering together of the waters called he Seas: and God saw that it was good.

And God said, Let the earth bring forth grass, the herb yielding seed, and the fruit tree yielding fruit after his kind, whose seed is in itself, upon the earth: and it was so.

And the earth brought forth grass, and herb yielding seed after his kind, and the tree yielding fruit, whose seed was in itself, after his kind: and God saw that it was good.

And the evening and the morning were the third day.

And God said, Let there be lights in the firmament of the heaven to divide the day from the night; and let them be for signs, and for seasons, and for days, and years:

And let them be for lights in the firmament of the heaven to give light upon the earth: and it was so.

And God made two great lights; the greater light to rule the day, and the lesser light to rule the night: he made the stars also.

And God set them in the firmament of the heaven to give light upon the earth,

And to rule over the day and over the night, and to divide the light from the darkness: and God saw that it was good.

And the evening and the morning were the fourth day.

And God said, Let the waters bring forth abundantly the moving creature that hath life, and fowl that may fly above the earth in the open firmament of heaven.

And God created great whales, and every living creature that moveth, which the waters brought forth abundantly, after their kind, and every winged fowl after his kind: and God saw that it was good.

And God blessed them, saying, Be fruitful, and multiply, and fill the waters in the seas, and let fowl multiply in the earth.

And the evening and the morning were the fifth day.

And God said, Let the earth bring forth the living creature after his kind, cattle, and creeping thing, and beast of the earth after his kind: and it was so.

And God made the beast of the earth after his kind, and cattle after their kind, and every thing that creepeth upon the earth after his kind: and God saw that it was good.

And God said, Let us make man in our image, after our likeness: and let them have dominion over the fish of the sea, and over the fowl of the air, and over the cattle, and over all the earth, and over every creeping thing that creepeth upon the earth.

So God created man in his own image, in the image of God created he him; male and female created he them.

And God blessed them, and God said unto them, Be fruitful, and multiply, and replenish the earth, and subdue it: and have dominion over the fish of the sea, and over the fowl of the air, and over every living thing that moveth upon the earth.

And God said, Behold, I have given you every herb bearing seed, which is upon the face of all the earth, and every tree, in the which is the fruit of a tree yielding seed; to you it shall be for meat.

And to every beast of the earth, and to every fowl of the air, and to every thing that creepeth upon the earth, wherein there is life, I have given every green herb for meat: and it was so.

And God saw every thing that he had made, and, behold, it was very good. And the evening and the morning were the sixth day.

CHAPTER 2

Thus the heavens and the earth were finished, and all the host of them.

And on the seventh day God ended his work which he had made; and he rested on the seventh day from all his work which he had made.

And God blessed the seventh day, and sanctified it: because that in it he had rested from all his work which God created and made.

These are the generations of the heavens and of the earth when they were created, in the day that the LORD God made the earth and the heavens,

And every plant of the field before it was in the earth, and every herb of the field before it grew: for the LORD God had not caused it to rain upon the earth, and there was not a man to till the ground.

But there went up a mist from the earth, and watered the whole face of the ground.

And the LORD God formed man of the dust of the ground, and breathed into his nostrils the breath of life; and man became a living soul.

And the LORD God planted a garden eastward in Eden; and there he put the man whom he had formed.

And out of the ground made the LORD God to grow every tree that is pleasant to the sight, and good for food; the tree of life also in the midst of the garden, and the tree of knowledge of good and evil.

And a river went out of Eden to water the garden; and from thence it was parted, and became into four heads.

The name of the first is Pison: that is it which compasseth the whole land of Havilah, where there is gold;

And the gold of that land is good: there is bdellium and the onyx stone.

And the name of the second river is Gihon: the same is it that compasseth the whole land of Ethiopia.

And the name of the third river is Hiddekel: that is it which goeth toward the east of Assyria. And the fourth river is Euphrates.

And the LORD God took the man, and put him into the garden of Eden to dress it and to keep it.

And the LORD God commanded the man, saying, Of every tree of the garden thou mayest freely eat:

But of the tree of the knowledge of good and evil, thou shalt not eat of it: for in the day that thou eatest thereof thou shalt surely die.

And the LORD God said, It is not good that the man should be alone; I will make him an help meet for him.

And out of the ground the LORD God formed every beast of the field, and every fowl of the air; and brought them unto Adam to see what he would call them: and whatsoever Adam called every living creature, that was the name thereof.

And Adam gave names to all cattle, and to the fowl of the air, and to every beast of the field; but for Adam there was not found an help meet for him.

And the LORD God caused a deep sleep to fall upon Adam and he slept: and he took one of his ribs, and closed up the flesh instead thereof;

And the rib, which the LORD God had taken from man, made he a woman, and brought her unto the man.

And Adam said, This is now bone of my bones, and flesh of my flesh: she shall be called Woman, because she was taken out of Man.

Therefore shall a man leave his father and his mother, and shall cleave unto his wife: and they shall be one flesh.

And they were both naked, the man and his wife, and were not ashamed.

CHAPTER 3

Now the serpent was more subtil than any beast of the field which the LORD God had made. And he said unto the woman, Yea, hath God said, Ye shall not eat of every tree of the garden?

And the woman said unto the serpent, We may eat of the fruit of the trees of the garden:

But of the fruit of the tree which is in the midst of the garden, God hath said, Ye shall not eat of it, neither shall ye touch it, lest ye die.

And the serpent said unto the woman, Ye shall not surely die:

For God doth know that in the day ye eat thereof, then your eyes shall be opened, and ye shall be as gods, knowing good and evil.

And when the woman saw that the tree was good for food, and that it was pleasant to the eyes, and a tree to be desired to make one wise, she took of the fruit thereof, and did eat, and gave also unto her husband with her; and he did eat.

And the eyes of them both were opened, and they knew that they were naked; and they sewed fig leaves together, and made themselves aprons.

And they heard the voice of the LORD God walking in the garden in the cool of the day: and Adam and his wife hid themselves from the presence of the LORD God amongst the trees of the garden.

And the LORD God called unto Adam, and said unto him, Where art thou?

And he said, I heard thy voice in the garden, and I was afraid, because I was naked; and I hid myself.

And he said, Who told thee that thou wast naked? Hast thou eaten of the tree, whereof I commanded thee that thou shouldest not eat?

And the man said, The woman whom thou gavest to be with me, she gave me of the tree, and I did eat.

And the LORD God said unto the woman, What is this that thou hast done? And the woman said, The serpent beguiled me, and I did eat.

And the LORD God said unto the serpent, Because thou hast done this, thou art cursed above all cattle, and above every beast of the field; upon thy belly shalt thou go, and dust shalt thou eat all the days of thy life:

And I will put enmity between thee and the woman, and between thy seed and her seed; it shall bruise thy head, and thou shalt bruise his heel.

Unto the woman he said, I will greatly multiply thy sorrow and thy conception; in sorrow thou shalt bring forth children; and thy desire shall be to thy husband, and he shall rule over thee.

And unto Adam he said, Because thou hast hearkened unto the voice of thy wife, and hast eaten of the tree, of which I commanded thee, saying, Thou shalt not eat of it: cursed is the ground for thy sake; in sorrow shalt thou eat of it all the days of thy life;

Thorns also and thistles shall it bring forth to thee; and thou shalt eat the herb of the field;

In the sweat of thy face shalt thou eat bread, till thou return unto the ground; for out of it wast thou taken: for dust thou art, and unto dust shalt thou return.

And Adam called his wife's name Eve; because she was the mother of all living.

Unto Adam also and to his wife did the LORD God make coats of skins, and clothed them.

And the LORD God said, Behold, the man is become as one of us, to know good and evil: and now, lest he put forth his hand, and take also of the tree of life, and eat, and live for ever:

Therefore the LORD God sent him forth from the garden of Eden, to till the ground from whence he was taken.

So he drove out the man; and he placed at the east of the garden of Eden Cherubims, and a flaming sword which turned every way, to keep the way of the tree of life.

10 LEGENDARY ORIGINS

THE ORIGIN OF THE WREKIN (ENGLAND)

Long, long ago, in the days when there were giants in the land, two of them were turned out by the rest and forced to go and live by themselves, so they set to work to build themselves a hill to live in. In a very short time they had dug out the earth from the bed of the Severn, which runs in the trench they made to the present time, and with it they piled up the Wrekin, intending to make it their home.

Those bare patches on the turf, between the Bladderstone and the top of the hill, are the marks of their feet, where from that day to this the grass has never grown. But they had not been there long before they quarrelled, and one of them struck at the other with his spade, but failed to hit him, and the spade descending to the ground cleft the solid rock and made the "Needle's Eye."

Then they began to fight, and the giant with the spade (for they seem to have had only one between them -- perhaps that was what they quarrelled about!) was getting the best of it at first, but a raven flew up and pecked at his eyes, and the pain made him shed such a mighty tear that it hollowed out the little basin in the rock which we call the Raven's Bowl, or sometimes the Cuckoo's Cup, which has never been dry since, but is always full of water even in the hottest summers.

And now you may suppose that it was very easy for the other giant to master the one who had the spade, and when he had done so, he determined to put him where he could never trouble anyone again. So he very quickly built up the Ercall Hill beside the Wrekin, and imprisoned his fallen foe within it. There the poor blind giant remains until this day, and in the dead of night you may sometimes hear him groaning.

There is another and a better-known legend of this famous Wreken:

Once upon a time there was a wicked old giant in Wales who, for some reason or other, had a very great spite against the Mayor of Shrewsbury and all his people, and he made up his mind to dam up the Severn, and by that means cause such a flood that the town would be drowned.

So off he set, carrying a spadeful of earth, and tramped along mile after mile trying to find the way to Shrewsbury. And how he missed it I cannot tell, but he must have gone wrong somewhere, for at last he got close to Wellington, and by that time he was puffing and blowing under his heavy load, and wishing he was at the end of his journey. By and by there came a cobbler along the road with a sack of old boots and shoes on his back, for he lived at Wellington, and went once a fortnight to Shrewsbury to collect his customers' old boots and shoes, and take them home with him to mend.

And the giant called out to him. "I say," he said, "how far is it to Shrewsbury?"

"Shrewsbury?" said the cobbler; "what do you want at Shrewsbury?"

"Why," said the giant, "to fill up the Severn with this lump of earth I've got here. I've an old grudge against the mayor and the folks at Shrewsbury, and now I mean to drown them out, and get rid of them all at once."

"My word!" thought the cobbler. "This'll never do! I can't afford to lose my customers!" And he spoke up again. "Eh!" he said, "you'll never get to Shrewsbury -- not today nor tomorrow. Why look at me! I'm just come from Shrewsbury, and I've had time to wear out all these old boots and shoes on the road since I started." And he showed him his sack.

"Oh!" said the giant, with a great groan. "Then it's no use! I'm fairly tired out already, and I can't carry this load of mine any farther. I shall just drop it here and go back home."

So he dropped the earth on the ground just where he stood, and scraped his boots on the spade, and off he went home again to Wales, and nobody ever heard anything of him in Shropshire after. But where he put down his load, there stands the Wrekin to this day; and even the earth that he scraped off his boots was such a pile that it made the little Ercall by the Wrekin's side.

BOMERE POOL (ENGLAND)

Notes on the legend:
Bomere Pool is a lake near Shrewsbury in western England. The word mere (akin to the German Meer, sea) can refer to a sea, an inlet, or a lake.

Many years ago a village stood in the hollow which is now filled up by the mere. But the inhabitants were a wicked race, who mocked at God and his priest. They turned back to the idolatrous practices of their fathers, and worshipped Thor and Woden. They scorned to bend the knee, save in mockery, to the White Christ who had died to save their souls.

The old priest earnestly warned them that God would punish such wickedness as theirs by some sudden judgment, but they laughed him to scorn. They fastened fish bones to the skirt of his cassock, and set the children to pelt him with mud and stones. The holy man was not dismayed at this; nay, he renewed his entreaties and warnings, so that some few turned from their evil ways and worshipped with him in the little chapel which stood on the bank of a rivulet that flowed down from the mere on the hillside.

The rains fell that December in immense quantities. The mere was swollen beyond its usual limits, and all the hollows in the hills were filled to overflowing. One day when the old priest was on the hillside gathering fuel he noticed that the barrier of peat, earth, and stones, which prevented the mere from flowing into the valley, was apparently giving way before the mass of water above. He hurried down to the village and besought the men to come up and cut a channel for the discharge of the superfluous waters of the mere. They only greeted his proposal with shouts of derision, and told him to go and mind his prayers, and not spoil their feast with his croaking and his killjoy presence.

These heathen were then keeping their winter festival with great revelry. It fell on Christmas Eve. The same night the aged priest summoned his few faithful ones to attend at the midnight mass, which ushered in the feast of our Savior's nativity. The night was stormy, and the rain fell in torrents, yet this did not prevent the little flock from coming to the chapel. The old servant of God had already begun the holy sacrifice, when a roar was heard in the upper part of the valley. The server was just ringing the Sanctus bell which hung in the bell cot, when a flood of water dashed into the church, and rapidly rose till it put out the altar lights. In a few moments more the whole building was washed away, and the mere, which had burst its mountain barrier, occupied the hollow in which the village had stood.

Men say that if you sail over the mere on Christmas Eve, just after midnight, you may hear the Sanctus bell tolling.

Here is another variant of the same legend, related to me by a lady in the parish of Condover, 1881:

In the days of the Roman empire, when Uriconium was standing, a very wicked city stood where we now see Bomere Pool. The inhabitants had turned back from Christianity to heathenism, and though God sent one of the Roman soldiers to be a prophet to them, like Jonah to Nineveh, they would not repent. Far from that, they ill-used and persecuted the preacher.

Only the daughter of the governor remained constant to the faith. She listened gladly to the Christian's teaching, and he on his part loved her, and would have had her to be his wife. But no such happy lot was in store for the faithful pair. On the following Easter eve, sudden destruction came upon the city. The distant Caradoc [a hill] sent forth flames of fire, and at the same time the city was overwhelmed by a tremendous flood, while the sun in the heavens danced for joy, and the cattle in the stalls knelt in thanksgiving that God had not permitted such wickedness to go unpunished.

But the Christian warrior was saved from the flood, and he took a boat and rowed over the waters, seeking for his betrothed, but all in vain. His boat was overturned, and he too was drowned in the depths of the mere. Yet whenever Easter eve falls on the same day as it did that year, the form of the Roman warrior may be seen again, rowing across Bomere in search of his lost love, while the church bells are heard ringing far in the depths below.

THE ORIGIN OF TIS LAKE (DENMARK)

A troll had once taken up his abode near the village of Kund, in the high bank on which the church now stands; but when the people about there had become pious, and went constantly to church, the troll was dreadfully annoyed by their almost incessant ringing of bells in the steeple of the church. He was at last obliged, in consequence of it, to take his departure; for nothing has more contributed to the emigration of the troll folk out of the country than the increasing piety of the people, and their taking to bell ringing. The troll of Kund accordingly quitted the country, and went over to Funen, where he lived for some time in peace and quiet.

Now it chanced that a man who had lately settled in the town of Kund, coming to Funen on business, met on the road with this same troll. "Where do you live?" said the troll to him.

Now there was nothing whatever about the troll unlike a man, so he answered him, as was the truth, "I am from the town of Kund."

"So?" said the troll. "I don't know you then! And yet I think I know every man in Kund. Will you, however," continued he, "just be so kind to take a letter from me back with you to Kund?"

The man said, of course, he had no objection. The troll then thrust the letter into his pocket, and charged him strictly not to take it out till he came to Kund church, and then to throw it over the churchyard wall, and the person for whom it was intended would get it.

The troll then went away in great haste, and with him the letter went entirely out of the man's mind. But when he was come back to Zealand he sat down by the meadow where Tis Lake now is, and suddenly recollected the troll's letter. He felt a great desire to look at it at least. So he took it out of his pocket, and sat a while with it in his hands, when suddenly there began to dribble a little water out of the seal. The letter now unfolded itself, and the water came out faster and faster, and it was with the utmost difficulty that the poor man was enabled to save his life, for the malicious troll had enclosed an entire lake in the letter.

The troll, it is plain, had thought to avenge himself on Kund church by destroying it in this manner; but God ordered it so that the lake chanced to run out in the great meadow where it now flows.

GEFION CREATES THE ISLAND OF ZEALAND (FROM THE PROSE EDDA OF SNORRI STURLUSON)

King Gylfi ruled the lands that are now called Sweden. It is told of him that he gave a plow-land in his kingdom, the size four oxen could plow in a day and a night, to a beggar-woman as a reward for the way she had entertained him. This woman, however, was of the family of the Æsir. Her name was Gefion.

From the north of Giantland she took four oxen and yoked them to a plow, but those were her sons by a giant. The plow went in so hard and deep that it loosened the land and the oxen dragged it westwards into the sea, stopping in a certain sound. There Gefion set the land for good and gave it a name, calling it Zealand.

But the place where the land had been torn up was afterwards a lake. It is now known in Sweden as "The Lake." And there are as many bays in "The Lake" as there are headlands in Zealand.

As the poet Bragi the Old says:

> Gefion dragged with laughter
> from Gylfi liberal prince
> What made Denmark larger,
> so that beasts of draft
> the oxen reeked with sweat;
> four heads they had, eight eyes to boot
> who went before broad island-pasture
> ripped away as loot.

GEFION CREATES THE ISLAND OF ZEALAND (FROM THE YNGLINDA SAGA OF SNORRI STURLUSON)

When Odin looked into the future and worked magic, he knew that his offspring would dwell and till in the northern parts of the earth. He, therefore, set his brothers Ve and Vili over Asagarth [in the land of the Turks] and he himself went away and with him went all the priests and many of his folk. First he went to Gardarik [Russia] and from there he went south to Saxland [Germany]. He had many sons; he won kingdoms far over Saxland and set his sons as rulers over them.

From there he fared north to the sea and found himself a dwelling on an island which is now called Odensö in Fyn [Funen]. Then he sent Gefion northeast over the sound to look for land; she then came to Gylfi, who gave her a plow-land. Next she went to a giant's home and there begot four sons with a giant. She shaped them in the likeness of oxen, yoked them to a plow and broke up the land into the sea westwards opposite Odensö; it was called Selund [an old spelling for Zealand], and there she dwelt afterwards.

Skjold, Odin's son, took her to wife and they lived in Leidra. There where she plowed is now a lake or sea called Löginn; the fjords in Löginn answer to the nesses in Selund.

Thus said Bragi the Old:

> Gefion drew with gladness
> From the gold-rich Gylfi
> Denmark's new increase
> (So that it reeked from the beasts).
> The oxen bore eight eyes
> And four heads.
> There they went forth,
> Far over Vinö's bay.

Notes on the legend:
Odin's name is still carried by the Danish island of Fyn's most important city, Odense, the birthplace of Hans Christian Andersen.

Leidre, also spelled Leire or Lejre is near Roskilde on the island of Zealand. Today it is the site of a reconstructed iron age village.

Odin's son Skjold who married Gefion is said to be the founder of the Danish Skjoldung royal dynasty and is identified with Scyld Sceafing mentioned in Beowulf.

THE ORIGIN OF THE ISLAND HIDDENSEE (GERMANY)

When in the ninth century the monks of Corvei were attempting to convert the heathens of Rügen to the Christian faith, one of the missionaries traveled to Hiddensee. Late one evening he stopped at the door of a hut in a fishing village and asked to be allowed inside. The woman of the house rejected him as a beggar, sending him away with harsh words. He then turned to her poor neighbor, where he at once received shelter and nourishment.

The next morning he thanked the poor widow, then departed from her with these words, "I have neither gold nor silver to pay for the lodging, but the first thing you do today shall be blessed!"

Thinking nothing of these words, she began to measure a little piece of linen that she had woven. But it had no end. She measured and measured throughout the whole day, until the sun went down, and thus filled her entire house with linen. Remembering the words of the apostle, she revealed the source of her good fortune to her envious neighbor.

The latter remembered the words exactly, and when, some time later, the missionary once again knocked on her door, she received him with the greatest eagerness.

The next morning, after the guest had departed saying the familiar words, she decided to immediately count the money she had saved in a jar. However, first of all she had to go outside to answer an unexpected call of nature. Suddenly the holy man's blessing took effect, and with such force that the land was flooded and became separated from Rügen.

11 THE ORIGIN OF UNDERGROUND PEOPLE: LEGENDS ABOUT ELVES AND OTHER HIDDEN CREATURES

ORIGIN OF THE HIDDEN PEOPLE (TWO LEGENDS FROM ICELAND)

I.

Once upon a time, God Almighty came to visit Adam and Eve. They received him with joy, and showed him everything they had in the house. They also brought their children to him, to show him, and these He found promising and full of hope.

Then He asked Eve whether she had no other children than these whom she now showed him.

She said "None."

But it so happened that she had not finished washing them all, and, being ashamed to let God see them dirty, had hidden the unwashed ones. This God knew well, and said therefore to her, "What man hides from God, God will hide from man."

These unwashed children became forthwith invisible, and took up their abode in mounds, and hills, and rocks. From these are the elves descended, but we men from those of Eve's children whom she had openly and frankly shown to God. And it is only by the will and desire of the elves themselves that men can ever see them.

II.

A traveler once lost his way, and knew not whither to turn or what to do. At last, after wandering about for some time, he came to a hut, which he had never seen before; and on his knocking at the door, an old woman opened it, and invited him to come in, which he gladly did.

Inside, the house seemed to be a clean and good one. The old woman led him to the warmest room, where were sitting two young and beautiful girls. Besides these, no one else was in the house. He was well received and kindly treated, and having eaten a good supper was shown to bed.

He asked whether one of the girls might stay with him, as his companion for the night, and his request was granted.

And now wishing to kiss her, the traveler turned towards her, and placed his hand upon her; but his hand sank through her, as if she had been of mist, and though he could well see her lying beside him, he could grasp nothing but the air.

So he asked what this all meant, and she said, "Be not astonished, for I am a spirit. When the devil, in times gone by, made war in heaven, he, with all his armies, was driven into outer darkness. Those who turned their eyes to look after him as he fell, were also driven out of heaven; but those who were neither for nor against him, were sent to the earth and commanded to dwell there in the rocks and mountains.

These are called elves and hidden people. They can live in company with none but their own race. They do either good or evil, which they will, but what they do they do thoroughly. They have no bodies as you other mortals, but can take a human form and be seen of men when they wish. I am one of these fallen spirits, and so you can never hope to embrace me."

To this fate the traveler yielded himself, and has handed down to us this story.

THE ORIGIN OF BERGFOLK (DENMARK)

Bergmen originated in this way, that when Our Lord cast down the wicked angels from heaven they could not all get to hell together, and some of them settled in the mounds and banks.

Brownies, bergmen, and such creatures originated in this way. When Our Lord cast the wicked angels down from heaven some of them fell on mounds and banks, and these became bergmen; some fell into woods and mosses, and these became fairies (ellefolk), while those that fell into buildings became brownies (nisser). They are just little devils, the whole lot of them.

WHEN SATAN WAS CAST OUT OF HEAVEN (SWEDEN)

Know that when Satan was cast out of heaven, on account of his pride, and fell to the earth, there were other spirits, which, like him, were also cast out. These spirits, in their fall, were borne hither and thither on the winds like the golden leaves in the autumn storm, falling to earth finally, some into the sea, some into the forests, and some upon the mountains. Where they fell there they remained, so the saying runs, and found there their field of action. After their abiding places they were given different names. Thus we have sea nymphs, mountain fairies, wood fairies, elves, and other spirits, all of which are described in the catechism.

ORIGIN OF THE UNDERGROUND PEOPLE IN AMRUM (GERMANY)

The Lord Jesus came one day to a house where a woman lived who had five beautiful and five ugly children. She hid the five ugly children in the cellar. The Lord Jesus asked her where her other children were. The woman said: "I do not have any more children."

Then the Lord Jesus cursed the five ugly children, saying: "That which is beneath shall remain beneath, and that which above shall remain above!"

When the woman returned to the cellar, her five ugly children had disappeared. The underground people are their descendants.

LOWER ELEMENTAL SPIRITS (BOHEMIA)

In addition to the gods, heathens knew a whole row of lower demons which can be placed together under the names sprites and elves. They constitute a distinct spirit realm on earth, independent of the world of humans. They possess supernatural powers with which they harm and help humans. However, they shy away from humans, because physically they are not our equals. In Bohemia they tell about the origin of these demons as follows:

When God cast out the arrogant angels from heaven, they became the evil spirits that plague mankind day and night, tormenting us and inflicting us with harm. The ones who fell into hell and into caves and abysses became devils and death-maidens. However, those who fell onto the earth became goblins, imps, dwarfs, thumblings, alps, noon-and-evening-ghosts, and will-o'-the-wisps. Those who fell into the forests became the wood-spirits who live there: the hey-men, the wild-men, the forest-men, the wild-women, and the forest-women. Finally, those who fell into the water became water spirits: water-men, mermaids, and merwomen.

ORIGIN OF THE FAIRIES (ANGLESEA, WALES)

In our Savior's time there lived a woman whose fortune it was to be possessed of nearly a score of children, and as she saw our blessed Lord approach her dwelling, being ashamed of being so prolific, and that he might not see them all, she concealed about half of them closely, and after his departure, when she went in search of them, to her great surprise found they were all gone. They never afterwards could be discovered, for it was supposed that as a punishment from heaven for hiding what God had given her, she was deprived of them; and it is said these her offspring have generated the race called fairies.

THE FAIRIES AS FALLEN ANGELS (IRELAND)

The islanders, like all the Irish, believe that the fairies are the fallen angels who were cast down by the Lord God out of heaven for their sinful pride. And some fell into the sea, and some on the dry land, and some fell deep down into hell, and the devil gives to these knowledge and power, and sends them on earth where they work much evil.

But the fairies of the earth and the sea are mostly gentle and beautiful creatures, who will do no harm if they are let alone, and allowed to dance on the fairy raths in the moonlight to their own sweet music, undisturbed by the presence of mortals.

As a rule, the people look on fire as the great preservative against witchcraft, for the devil has no power except in the dark. So they put a live coal under the chum, and they wave a lighted wisp of straw above the cow's head if the beast seems sickly. But as to the pigs, they take no trouble, for they say the devil has no longer any power over them now. When they light a candle they cross themselves, because the evil spirits are then clearing out of the house in fear of the light, lire and Holy Water they hold to be sacred, and are powerful; and the best safeguard against all things evil, and the surest test in case of suspected witchcraft.

12 EVE'S UNEQUAL CHILDREN (GERMANY, JACOB AND WILHELM GRIMM)

When Adam and Eve were driven from paradise, they were forced to build a house for themselves on barren ground, and eat their bread by the sweat of their brow. Adam hoed the field, and Eve spun the wool. Every year Eve brought a child into the world, but the children were unlike each other. Some were good looking, and some ugly.

After a considerable time had gone by, God sent an angel to them to announce that he himself was coming to inspect their household. Eve, delighted that the Lord should be so gracious, cleaned her house diligently, decorated it with flowers, and spread rushes on the floor. Then she brought in her children, but only the good-looking ones. She washed and bathed them, combed their hair, put freshly laundered shirts on them, and cautioned them to be polite and well-behaved in the presence of the Lord. They were to bow down before him courteously, offer to shake hands, and to answer his questions modestly and intelligently.

The ugly children, however, were not to let themselves be seen. She hid one of them beneath the hay, another in the attic, the third in the straw, the fourth in the stove, the fifth in the cellar, the sixth under a tub, the seventh beneath the wine barrel, the eighth under an old pelt, the ninth and tenth beneath the cloth from which she made their clothes, and the eleventh and twelfth under the leather from which she cut their shoes.

She had just finished when someone knocked at the front door. Adam looked through a crack, and saw that it was the Lord. He opened the door reverently, and the Heavenly Father entered. There stood the good-looking children all in a row. They bowed before him, offered to shake hands, and knelt down.

The Lord began to bless them. He laid his hands on the first, saying, "You shall be a powerful king," did the same thing to the second, saying, "You a prince," to the third, "You a count," to the fourth, "You a knight," to the fifth, "You a nobleman," to the sixth, "You a burgher," to the seventh, "You a merchant," to the eighth, "You a scholar." Thus he bestowed his richest blessings upon them all.

When Eve saw that the Lord was so mild and gracious, she thought, "I will bring forth my ugly children as well. Perhaps he will bestow his blessings on them too." So she ran and fetched them from the hay, the straw, the stove, and wherever else they were hidden away. In they came, the whole coarse, dirty, scabby, sooty lot of them.

The Lord smiled, looked at them all, and said, "I will bless these as well."

He laid his hands on the first and said to him, "You shall be a peasant," to the second, "You a fisherman," to the third, "You a smith," to the fourth, "You a tanner," to the fifth, "You a weaver," to the sixth, "You a shoemaker," to the seventh, "You a tailor," to the eighth, "You a potter," to the ninth, "You a teamster," to the tenth, "You a sailor," to the eleventh, "You a messenger," to the twelfth, "You a household servant, all the days of your life."

When Eve had heard all this she said, "Lord, how unequally you divide your blessings. All of them are my children, whom I have brought into the world. You should favor them all equally."

But God replied, "Eve, you do not understand. It is right and necessary that the entire world should be served by your children. If they were all princes and lords, who would plant grain, thresh it, grind and bake it? Who would forge iron, weave cloth, build houses, plant crops, dig ditches, and cut out and sew clothing? Each shall stay in his own place, so that one shall support the other, and all shall be fed like the parts of a body."

Then Eve answered, "Oh, Lord, forgive me, I spoke too quickly to you. Let your divine will be done with my children as well."

13 THE NORSE CREATION MYTH (FROM THE PROSE EDDA OF SNORRI STURLUSON)

Muspell
The first world to exist was Muspell, a place of light and heat whose flames are so hot that those who are not native to that land cannot endure it.

Surt sits at Muspell's border, guarding the land with a flaming sword. At the end of the world he will vanquish all the gods and burn the whole world with fire.

Ginnungagap and Niflheim
Beyond Muspell lay the great and yawning void named Ginnungagap, and beyond Ginnungagap lay the dark, cold realm of Niflheim.

Ice, frost, wind, rain and heavy cold emanated from Niflheim, meeting in Ginnungagap the soft air, heat, light, and soft air from Muspell.

Ymir
Where heat and cold met appeared thawing drops, and this running fluid grew into a giant frost ogre named Ymir.

Frost ogres
Ymir slept, falling into a sweat. Under his left arm there grew a man and a woman. And one of his legs begot a son with the other. This was the beginning of the frost ogres.

Audhumla
Thawing frost then became a cow called Audhumla. Four rivers of milk ran from her teats, and she fed Ymir.

Buri, Bor, and Bestla
The cow licked salty ice blocks. After one day of licking, she freed a man's hair from the ice. After two days, his head appeared. On the third day the whole man was there. His name was Buri, and he was tall, strong, and handsome.

Buri begot a son named Bor, and Bor married Bestla, the daughter of a giant.

Odin, Vili, and Vé
Bor and Bestla had three sons: Odin was the first, Vili the second, and Vé the third.

It is believed that Odin, in association with his brothers, is the ruler of heaven and earth. He is the greatest and most famous of all men.

The death of Ymir
Odin, Vili, and Vé killed the giant Ymir.

When Ymir fell, there issued from his wounds such a flood of blood, that all the frost ogres were drowned, except for the giant Bergelmir who escaped with his wife by climbing onto a lur [a hollowed-out tree trunk that could serve either as a boat or a coffin]. From them spring the families of frost ogres.

Earth, trees, and mountains
The sons of Bor then carried Ymir to the middle of Ginnungagap and made the world from him. From his blood they made the sea and the lakes; from his flesh the earth; from his hair the trees; and from his bones the mountains. They made rocks and pebbles from his teeth and jaws and those bones that were broken.

Dwarfs
Maggots appeared in Ymir's flesh and came to life. By the decree of the gods they acquired human understanding and the appearance of men, although they lived in the earth and in rocks.

Sky, clouds, and stars

From Ymir's skull the sons of Bor made the sky and set it over the earth with its four sides. Under each corner they put a dwarf, whose names are East, West, North, and South.

The sons of Bor flung Ymir's brains into the air, and they became the clouds.

Then they took the sparks and burning embers that were flying about after they had been blown out of Muspell, and placed them in the midst of Ginnungagap to give light to heaven above and earth beneath. To the stars they gave appointed places and paths.

The earth was surrounded by a deep sea. The sons of Bor gave lands near the sea to the families of giants for their settlements.

Midgard

To protect themselves from the hostile giants, the sons of Bor built for themselves an inland stonghold, using Ymir's eyebrows. This stonghold they named Midgard.

Ask and Embla

While walking along the sea shore the sons of Bor found two trees, and from them they created a man and a woman.

Odin gave the man and the woman spirit and life. Vili gave them understanding and the power of movement. Vé gave them clothing and names. The man was named Ask [Ash] and the woman Embla [Elm]. From Ask and Embla have sprung the races of men who lived in Midgard.

Asgard

In the middle of the world the sons of Bor built for themselves a stronghold named Asgard, called Troy by later generations. The gods and their kindred lived in Asgard, and many memorable events have happened there.

In Asgard was a great hall named Hlidskjálf. Odin sat there on a high seat. From there he could look out over the whole world and see what everyone was doing. He understood everything that he saw.

Odin, Frigg, and the Æsir

Odin married Frigg, the daughter of Fjörgvin. From this family has come all the kindred that inhabited ancient Asgard and those kingdoms that belonged to it. Members of this family are called the Æsir, and they are all divinities. This must be the reason why Odin is called All-Father. He is the father of all the gods and men and of everything that he and his power created.

Thor

The earth was Odin's daughter and his wife as well. By her he had his first son, Thor. Might and strength were Thor's characteristics. By these he dominates every living creature.

Bifröst

As all informed people know, the gods built a bridge from earth to heaven called Bifröst. Some call it the rainbow. It has three colors and is very strong, made with more skill and cunning than other structures. But strong as it is, it will break when the sons of Muspell ride out over it. The gods are not to blame that this structure will then break. Bifröst is a good bridge, but there is nothing in this world that can be relied on when the sons of Muspell are on the warpath.

Yggdrasil

The chief sanctuary of the gods is by the ash tree Yggdrasil. There they hold their daily court. Yggdrasil is the best and greatest of all trees. Its branches spread out over the whole world and reach up over heaven.

ABOUT THE AUTHOR

Michelle McLaughlin is the co-founder of The McLaughlin Group and the author and editor of the series Fairy Tales the World Over. In addition, she writes books about specific legends and themes in fairy tales, and edits anthologies of classic works, both fiction and non-fiction.

There are currently eight books in the Fairy Tales the World Over series: The Emerald Fairy Book, The Amethyst Fairy Book, The Diamond Fairy Book, The Ruby Fairy Book, The Topaz Fairy Book, The Pearl Fairy Book, The Moonstone Fairy Book, and The Sapphire Fairy Book.

Michelle lives in Denton, Texas with her husband Adam and their three cats Neptune, Clementine, and Prunesquallor. She is a librarian at a junior college and enjoys cross-stitching.

Lightning Source UK Ltd.
Milton Keynes UK
UKHW021532241022
411005UK00011B/1793